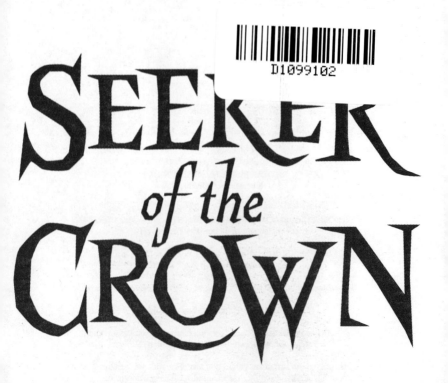

SEEKER of the CROWN

RUTH LAUREN

BLOOMSBURY
CHILDREN'S BOOKS
LONDON   OXFORD   NEW YORK   NEW DELHI   SYDNEY

BLOOMSBURY CHILDREN'S BOOKS
Bloomsbury Publishing Plc
50 Bedford Square, London WC1B 3DP, UK

BLOOMSBURY, BLOOMSBURY CHILDREN'S BOOKS and the Diana logo
are trademarks of Bloomsbury Publishing Plc

First published in the USA in 2018 by Bloomsbury Children's Books
1385 Broadway, New York, New York 10018

This edition published in Great Britain in 2018 by Bloomsbury Publishing Plc

A catalogue record for this book is available from the British Library

ISBN: TPB: 978-1-4088-8456-0; eBook: 978-1-4088-8457-7

2 4 6 8 10 9 7 5 3 1

Typeset by Westchester Publishing Services

Printed and bound by CPI Group (UK) Ltd, Croydon, CR0 4YY

MIX
Paper from
responsible sources
FSC® C020471

To find out more about our authors and books visit www.bloomsbury.com
and sign up for our newsletters

To Elysia
This is for you, like everything else

CHAPTER 1

"Valor!"

My head jerks up, and the honey I was toying with falls in a sticky glob on to the golden tablecloth. A servant leaps forward to clean it up.

"Sorry, Mother."

Everyone at the long table in the Magadanskyan palace banquet hall looks at me. It feels just like having the eyes of the other inmates at Tyur'ma on me in the icy dining hall.

I duck my head, gazing at the fine china plate in front of me. All this food makes me think of Feliks and Katia, but I don't even know where my friends are.

"Valor." This time it's a low hiss, and Mother shakes her head, her eyes wide. I look down at the threads of the shining tapestry covering the table. More honey. I move my plate over the stain, and Mother's shoulders slump. She's sitting opposite me, next to the steward of Magadanskya, Lady Olegevna. Behind her is a raised dais with a large glass case resting on it. Inside, nestled on velvet as deep a purple as Lady Olegevna's gown, is the music box, displayed on our last night here in celebration of my sister returning it to its rightful owners.

Mother casts a worried glance at the grand double doors, not for the first time this evening. The first course has already been delayed because Father and Sasha aren't here. There's an empty seat next to me where my sister should be sitting, and another next to Mother where Father should be. They're late to our banquet. In fact, they've been busy together for much of the past month.

Thank the saints this is the last function to attend before we return to Demidova tomorrow. Although, since this particular banquet is in the Raisayevna family's honour, I could perhaps show a little more decorum as the elder daughter— even if I'm elder by only four minutes.

I was so happy when Mother asked permission for us to travel here with Father and Sasha so we would never have to be apart again. After all we'd been through, Queen Ana said yes, but now Mother's talking to Lady Olegevna as if *she* were Queen Ana's chief adviser, not Father, and I'm five seconds away from stabbing myself with my silver fork just so I can leave.

Mother's hand flutters about, and then goes to her throat. "I can't think what's keeping them. I'm so sorry. I'm sure they'll be here soon."

Lady Olegevna inclines her head graciously, but I can tell Mother's embarrassed.

I leap up, knocking into my chair a little. "I'll go and find them," I say, maybe a touch too eagerly.

"I'll send someone," says Lady Olegevna. As steward rather than Queen, she doesn't wear a *kokoshnik*, but her hair is piled into hundreds of tiny braids and shot through with pearls that shine in the candlelight.

"I can do it. I'd like to help. May I?" I look from her to my mother.

Mother opens her mouth, but hesitates. "Thank you, Valor," she finally says. "Don't be too long."

I try not to run on the way out, but I'm not certain I do a particularly good job of it.

I close the double doors behind me as quietly as I can, then take a big breath in the wide, empty hallway. I've been kept by Mother's side under one pretence or another for an entire month. Since the day we returned the music box to Lady Olegevna and Queen Ana told me that Princess Anastasia had escaped the dungeon she'd been sent to for framing my sister, I've had no more leeway than a pup on a short leash. I liked it at first. After missing Mother so much while I was locked up in Tyur'ma, it was nice to be near her all the time. But Sasha and I are thirteen. We're *apprenticed* already. I can't wait to start on the journey home tomorrow so I can get back to the estate. The sooner this banquet is over and done with, the sooner I can take out my bow.

I hurry down the hallway. The floors here are wooden, not like the mosaics and tiles in Demidova, and the soft indoor shoes we all have to wear rub at my feet in a way my boots never do. I kick them off and pick them up—the servants are all busy in the kitchens or the banquet hall, so there's no one to see.

I gain speed until I'm practically running down the hallways and through the expansive library, where I quickly cast about for Sasha but find only a couple of sleeping dogs. The palace is empty. I head for the hallway that contains Father's temporary office. I should have gone there right away, and it occurs to me only now that I'm going to look foolish—at best—if Father and Sasha arrive at the banquet hall before I return.

The Magadanskyan palace, unlike the white turrets and onion domes of Demidova, is blocky and low, spread out in a long, wide cross, and completely adorned in gold. I head to the left arm of the cross, where I know Lady Magadanskya conducts all official business, and where Father and Sasha have been working for much of the time we've been here. I'm flying down a narrow corridor when I hear a single word from inside one of the offices. I slide to a halt.

The word was "traitor".

And the voice was Father's.

I've just run past his office. I recognise it now, though the door looks the same as all the others in this hallway.

I back up and quieten my breathing, about to knock on the door.

". . . when no one in the city, least of all Queen Ana, has been any the wiser as to how she got out or where she went, it only makes sense. She is his sister, after all."

Father again. He has to be talking about Anastasia. And . . . her brother, Prince Anatol? Anatol helped me uncover Anastasia's crimes and free Sasha. How can *he* be a traitor? I lower my hand and tilt my head a little closer.

"What will happen to him?" asks Sasha. Her voice sounds the way I feel. After what Anatol did for Sasha and me, I'd do anything for him.

"He's to be banished," says a voice I don't recognise—a woman's voice, low and hard to hear. *Banished?*

"But to where?" asks Father. "When is this happening? My family and I can't leave tonight. There's a banquet. Lady Olegevna expects—"

The woman cuts him off, but I can't make out what she says. I press forward and almost push my head through the gap in the door. I catch a glimpse of her Demidovan Queen's Guard uniform but hear only the words "palace" and "midnight tomorrow night".

"We'll be back in Demidova before then," says Father, his black eyebrows drawn down. "But right now, we really can't delay Lady Olegevna any longer."

He looks at Sasha, and she nods. The guard bows and spins around smartly, and I turn tail and dash partway down the hallway, halting to pull my shoes on and start walking back towards Father's office. I shouldn't have been eavesdropping like that; Father wouldn't like it.

I hear them all say a few more things to one another, things I can't decipher at all, and then the guard exits the office, marching away down the hallway without a glance at me. Sasha and Father emerge.

"Valor!" says my sister. She sounds pleased to see me.

I smile. Strange to say, but even though the whole family came to Magadanskya so we could be together, I've barely seen her at all.

"I came to find you both," I say. "The banquet's already started."

Father nods. "We'd better hurry." He strides away on long legs, and Sasha and I scurry to keep up.

The crease between Sasha's eyebrows is almost as deep as Father's, but when she catches me looking, she smiles. "Are you looking forward to going home?"

I nod, surprised that this is what she asks. "I am. Is everything OK?"

She takes my hand as we jog to match Father's pace. "Of course. You know how it can be once we start in on discussions. I'm sorry you had to leave the banquet to find us."

Now it's my turn to frown. I didn't mind leaving the hall at all. Surely she knows that.

I lower my voice. Father's outstripped us anyway, despite our best efforts.

"Is everything all right in Demidova?"

Sasha stares at me for a second, her dark eyes wide, and then blinks. "Oh, you mean the Queen's Guard? Yes, of course. Just the weekly update—apparently Anatol's cousin Inessa is visiting. It's nothing. I know how much politics bore you. Come on, let's catch up with Father. I'm hungry."

She speeds up and I frown at her back, feeling a pinch of annoyance at the back of my throat. We discussed things as important as this right under Peacekeepers' noses in the laundry room at Tyur'ma—is it really so difficult now to tell me what's happened to Anatol?

I hurry after my sister and father. I should control my impatience better—once we're seated in the banquet hall, Sasha will tell me what she knows. But my mind races as my feet fly across the library floor. I never had the chance to see how Anatol took the news about his sister escaping; Queen Ana whisked him away after the music-box ceremony, and my father, as the queen's advisor and ambassador, was instructed to immediately travel to Magadanskya with Lady Olegevna and meet with the court there in Queen Ana's stead. She couldn't leave with Princess Anastasia missing.

I've thought of little else while I've been trapped in Magadanskya: who helped the princess escape? Where is she now? What will she do?

Now I add another question I can't answer: why is Anatol being banished?

As we reach the banquet hall, servants open the doors for us. Father holds up his hands and sweeps into the room, offering apologies and a joke at his own expense. When I look over at my sister, she's doing the same thing as she glides through the hall. I tug at the heels of my palace slippers.

By the time Father and Sasha take their seats, the whole company is smiling, and Lady Olegevna is summoning the first course of food. Sasha's face is as smooth and serene as a bronze statue.

I give her a pointed look. "Are you sure everything's OK?" We can talk in code if we need to; it wouldn't be the first time we've sat in a dining hall and passed secrets to each other.

"Yes, delicious," she says, taking a large bite of the soft, doughy bread a servant has placed in front of her.

"No one's listening to us," I say. "We can talk about anything." I don't even bother to whisper, because it's true: both Mother and Father are talking with Lady Olegevna, and no one is even looking at us.

"What do you want to talk about? Are you looking forward to going home?"

She already asked me that. My annoyance returns, but now it's mixed with disbelief. I keep thinking she's just being cautious, but as the evening wears on, with courses of meats and fruits and sparkling-cold ices and speeches and applause, she says nothing. As we pack up the last of our things before bed and bid each other goodnight, she says nothing. While we wait for the carriage to be loaded in the bright, cold sunshine the next morning, stamping our feet on the glittering snow, she says nothing. The journey back to Demidova stretches through the day and into dusk, and my heart gets smaller, my throat tighter.

She's going to keep it from me. She's not going to tell me Anatol's been arrested, not going to tell me he's been banished, or why. She's not going to say anything at all.

CHAPTER 2

I stare straight ahead without moving, my eyes trained on the small, unlit doorway across the street. We arrived back in Demidova only two hours ago, but I've already been hidden deep in the shadows at the mouth of this alley for twenty minutes.

Four months ago I faked an assassination attempt on the prince in order to get arrested and break Sasha out of Tyur'ma. Now I need to find out why the prince has been banished. But I'm wondering if I'm in the wrong place—if I should have lain in wait somewhere in the cobbled square where I could see the front entrance of the Demidovan palace through the golden gates instead.

I only know about this particular exit from Sasha, who collects these details of palace life, magpie-like, from our father. It's a little-known door usually used by visiting dignitaries who want to avoid the gaze of the general public during their meetings with the queen. I'm betting it's also being used for a far different purpose tonight. But I've been wrong before. Sasha doesn't tell me everything.

The clock tower chimes the twelve beats of midnight. I glance up, blinking, just to give my eyes a rest. I'm tired after travelling all day. The turrets and domes of the palace are bleached by starlight on this crisp, snow-covered night. Flakes fall out of the darkness, adding to the ankle-deep layer on the ground. A muffled noise snaps my attention back to the door. I lean forward, holding my breath.

The sound repeats—the quiet *snick* of a lock—and the door opens, pushing a small drift of snow in an arc. A cloaked figure scans the side street, then beckons behind. Others step out on to the unlit road—three of them following the first.

I draw back into the darkness, pressing against the rough stone of the wall as the four move past, quick and silent in their furred boots. I try to keep my breathing measured and even, but my heartbeat won't quieten, won't let me release the tension tightening every muscle in my frozen body. My crossbow is strapped to my back, just in case, and I reach up to touch its solid presence.

One of the figures is shorter than the others, though not by much. I inch forward to see his face, to see if it is really my friend. I catch a glimpse of dark hair, the profile of a straight nose, and nothing more, but it's enough.

Prince Anatol.

I let all four figures get almost to the bottom of the empty street before I slip out of the alley and follow, keeping to the shadows, hugging the walls of first the bank and then the furrier's.

I shift the bow on my back, angling it so it doesn't scrape against a wall and give me away. At the end of the street the four figures turn left, and I hurry after them, the soft snow compacting under my boots.

We go on for several turns, and I would be enjoying the chance to put my tracking training to good use if it weren't for the circumstances. All I wanted was to sink into my bed the way Mother and Father and Sasha did. My parents would be frantic if they found out I was here, but since Sasha wouldn't tell me what was happening, I had no choice but to sneak out of the house.

There's a sound behind me. I only hear it because I've paused to avoid a street lamp. It's the slight creak of a tread on new snow. My hand shoots up to the bow at my back. I glance ahead, only my eyes moving. The last cloaked guard of the four walks under the illumination of some tavern windows and disappears around a corner.

I weigh my options and dash forward, hoping the snow will muffle my footfalls. I can't lose sight of the prince now, even if someone else is following him.

My breath clouds the air as I reach the tavern, laughter and shouts drowning out any trace of noise behind me. I reach a crossroads as huge, thick snowflakes suddenly begin falling out of the night on to five narrow, cobbled lanes that spiderweb away from the intersection. I turn in a circle, blinking the snowfall away. A dull glint catches my eye down at the bottom of one of the lanes—a sword, maybe—and I take the chance, running flat-out. Keeping my cover isn't worth it if I lose track of the prince in what's rapidly becoming a blizzard.

Buildings press in on either side, wind whipping through the space between. I could be back in Tyur'ma, heading for the cell block in the harsh, cold grounds with my heart frozen inside me. I stop suddenly, breathing hard, and there it is again—a scuffle behind me. The sound of someone stopping themselves a pace too late.

I spin around, but the snowfall is fast and insistent and I see nothing, so I turn and charge on again, keeping the prince in sight, holding one hand up to shield my eyes. My legs are burning with cold now, but I go faster, dodging into the shadows outside a tall building with a chimney stack pushing grey smoke out against the snow.

I stop, skidding slightly into a drift, trying to get my bearings, and the person following me stops too.

The view ahead is obscured, but the path we're on is long and straight. The prince is far ahead of me, but the road is long enough that I have time to do something about my pursuer and still catch up to him—I hope.

I sidestep quickly to the right, ducking into the shadows, and jump up, clinging to the bottom of a fire escape for one precarious second before I haul myself up and on to it. Then I wait, hands stinging from gripping the cold metal.

A figure appears below me, moving hesitantly, peering into the swirling snow.

I can't see much—just the top of a dark *ushanka*—but even in thick furs the figure is slight. Smaller than me. But even if they weren't, I'm not about to let anyone stand in my way.

I hurl myself off the fire escape and drop on to the person below. They crumple to the ground with a grunt, and we both sink into calf-deep snow.

I scrabble at the furs beneath me as the person struggles. As they twist around, their *ushanka* falls off and a braid comes loose, a dark rope across the white ground. My hands go slack, and my pursuer throws me off so that I land on my backside in a drift.

"Sasha?"

"Yes. Sasha," says my sister, spitting snow. "And we need to hurry, or we're not going to make it through those gates before they close, and then we'll never get to speak to Prince Anatol."

I stare at her, and her cheeks flush darker as white flakes land on her hair. "What are you doing here? How did you even—?"

"I heard you sneaking out of the house. I don't sleep as soundly as I used to. Not since . . ." She frowns at the ground. "Valor, we really don't have time for this. Come on."

She struggles to her feet and offers me her hand. I take it, but slowly.

Sasha raises her eyebrows. "What makes you think you're the only one who wants to help the prince? Or at least find out what's going on. He did the same for me, didn't he? He believed I was innocent."

Heat rushes to my cold cheeks. Anatol always suspected Sasha was innocent of stealing the music box and that his own sister had been involved instead. For my part, I was so focused on getting Sasha out of Tyur'ma that I never stopped to consider whether she was guilty.

"You already know what's going on," I mutter.

Sasha shakes her head and then stops as understanding dawns on her face. "You were listening at the door, back in Magadanskya."

I cross my arms. "I came to find you. I can't help it if I overheard a few things."

Sasha's shoulders drop. "Valor, now that I'm working with Father, I can't tell you—I can't tell *anyone*—some of the things—"

"But it's *me*, Sasha. And this isn't just any old thing that has nothing to do with me. This is Anatol. I wish you hadn't come." Then I add, because that sounded too cruel even if part of me meant it, "It's not safe."

She sets her jaw and starts marching through the snow down the long road towards wherever Anatol is being taken. "No one is going to be safe until we find out what's going on in Demidova," she calls back to me.

"That's exactly why you should have told me," I mutter.

I brush the worst of the snow from my furs and rush after her. I might wish she weren't here, but I can't deny that she's right.

Sasha steps through the new snow, sinking deep each time she plants a boot. Soon we're both out of breath, but we still press on as fast as we can. Up ahead, there's a square of light, striped through with black. It takes me a second to realise I'm looking at railings in front of a window not too far down the lane.

Another patch of light appears, and then blurred shapes darken it: Prince Anatol and his escorts entering the house.

I nudge Sasha. She nods towards a tree, one of many dotting the gates of the large house. I nod back, and we both move to the side of the path, slipping behind the cover of the tree. Its bare branches are thick with snow, and they'll shield us, if only a little.

I peer out just as someone draws a heavy curtain across the window and all goes dark.

I shake my head. "I only got a glimpse, but they've already gone inside. There's one guard left outside. I think we should—Sasha?"

My sister steps out from behind the tree into plain sight. I reach for her, but she's already calling out, "Excuse me? Could you help me, please? I'm afraid I've got lost, with the blizzard as bad as it's been . . ." Her voice trails away, deadened to my ears by the snowfall. What is she doing? She didn't even warn me. I peek out and see the guard pointing away up the lane. Sasha's positioned herself so that the guard's back is to me.

I shove my annoyance aside and dash out, heading straight for the fence that surrounds the property. It stretches away as far as I can see in the dim light, around a house that's grander than I thought it would be. I haul myself up with stiff, cold hands, my heart beating even more violently with the sudden effort after such a long march through the snow.

I hang for a second at the top of the railing, the sharp prongs bruising me through my furs, and then I drop, hitting the ground on the other side and sending up a flurry of powder. I struggle upright, the shock of the landing still jarring my bones, and run in a crouch for the cover of the house.

I lose sight of Sasha as I speed along the right-hand wing, knee-deep in snow that's blown in drifts against the wall. I wish we'd agreed on a place to meet afterwards before she marched out like that.

My legs ache, and I'm slower and clumsier than I want to be, but I keep moving. I tug at three tall sash windows on the ground level, but all of them are locked, the drapes drawn. There has to be a back door, though.

I turn the corner just in time to see it open. I skid to a halt, throw myself back against the wall and peek out. A Queen's Guard, still wearing her dark cloak, sweeps a glance over the grounds of the house, and then shuts the door. Heavy bolts slide home, and a lock clicks. I slump against the cold stone and let out a big breath.

Maybe there are other entrances, other windows I haven't checked yet. I scour the grounds—empty and lacking any distinguishing features under the thick coating of snow. My boot hits something and I stumble forward, my hands hitting the ground with a hollow thump.

I scrape the snow away and find a cellar hatch. After a quick look around, I yank the handle. The door creaks and I have to pull hard, but it gives and opens on to a dark tunnel. I swing my legs into it, hoping to find steps. Instead I find a slide, and before I can grab the door, I slip down the sharp angle of it. My hands scrabble at the sides, my feet kicking out into the dark, but I can't halt my short and shocking descent. I land with a sudden *crack* in a cloud of dust, coughing as I draw in a breath.

I try to smother the noise, but the air is gritty and thick, coating my throat. So I push myself up, hands out, staring into the blackness of the cellar. I check my bow, and find it still strapped to my back. A thin strip of weak light shows high in one corner of the room, and I shuffle towards it.

My feet hit steps, and I have to slow even further, pushing each foot up and along every step to get to the light. I reach the door, feel around for a handle and find a knob that my frozen hand can barely grasp. I twist it and pull, blinking in the glowing firelight that comes through. It's the kitchen—mercifully empty at the moment. I listen over the blood rushing in my ears for signs of where the prince is being held. But I hear nothing.

I press on into a hallway, the skin on my face and hands stinging in the warmth of the house. A grand staircase sweeps up in front of me. Ahead there are three doors, all closed.

A panel under the stairs catches my eye—it's slightly ajar. I step across the polished floor and prise it open. Steps lead down, and I hear movement. There's someone in the room at the bottom. I have to take the chance; I can't leave Sasha waiting out in the freezing night for me, and I can't leave without finding Anatol.

I slip down the stairs, light on my feet, barely breathing. At the bottom is a big cage with a low door. Inside, Prince Anatol sits on an upturned wooden pail. He springs up when he sees me, his eyes wide. I rush to the bars at the same time he does.

"What are you doing here?" he whispers, his hands gripping the bars tightly.

"What am *I* doing here?" I ask. "What are *you* doing here? What happened?"

Anatol's gaze darts around. There are shadows under his eyes. He looks older, though it's only been a month since I last saw him.

"Anastasia found a way to implicate me in her treason. At least I assume she did. Who else could it be? Someone at court accused me of being in on her plan to steal the music box, and they arrested me. They said because I'm a boy and can never take the throne, Anastasia bribed me, offering me a position in her court that I'd never have while Mother reigned. They're saying I want Demidova to ally with Pyots'k like Anastasia does." He looks up at me, his grey eyes troubled. "They're saying I'm the one who helped her escape from the palace dungeon."

"So you're really going to be banished?" I ask. The cell he's in isn't even a cell—not for humans, anyway: it's a kennel for a dog, without even a bunk to sleep on. My voice comes out even quieter. "They're going to send you away? Forever?"

Prince Anatol opens his mouth to answer, but then his gaze flits up over my shoulder and he sucks in a breath. I whirl around, drawing my bow. Sasha stands in the dim light, a cloaked figure holding her by the shoulder.

CHAPTER 3

Within the space of a breath, I fit a bolt to my crossbow and send it flying true, pinning the stranger's cloak to the wall.

"Valor!" my sister cries out and starts forward. The cloaked figure wrenches his hood down, and my hands—ready to shoot again—falter.

Nicolai works the bolt out of the wall and from the material of his Guard uniform sleeve with a dark look at me. "Saints, will you stop doing that?" He strides across the room and shoves the bolt into my hand.

"Come with me now." His voice is grim, his face pinched with as much tension as when we escaped from Tyur'ma together.

"Where?" I demand. First Sasha follows me, and now Anatol's trusted guard is here?

"To the queen. She wanted to speak with you as soon as you returned to Demidova," says Nicolai. "Hurry. The other two guards are already suspicious." He gestures at Sasha. "I said I'd deal with this intruder myself before I returned to the barracks, but that won't keep them from checking down here for long, and we don't know if they can be trusted. We have to get out now."

I look at Prince Anatol. It's not right to see him like this, nor to leave him here. As though he knows what I'm thinking, he gives a firm nod. "Go."

I slot my bow back into place, and the three of us rush away up the stairs. Nicolai holds a warning hand out behind him, but the hallway is empty, and we head towards the back door. Nicolai hurries with the locks and pulls the door open wide as I glance behind us for signs of the other guards.

Outside, the wind has died down, the snowfall all but stopped, but the drifts are thick. Snow has piled in a wall outside the door. How far are we from the palace?

"This way," says Nicolai, pushing out into the cold night.

I wish I had breath to speak, to ask questions, but I'm already tired, and forcing my way through the snow saps the last of my energy. Nicolai leads us farther into the grounds, and I realise just how unlikely it was that we could have made it all the way back home only when I see the sledge with its dogs already harnessed and waiting by the fence.

First one, then the other five animals prick their ears and stand when they see us approach. Tongues loll out and breath huffs in front of thickly furred faces.

"You're lucky I hadn't already left," says Nicolai to us as we reach the sledge.

"What's going on here?" asks Sasha.

Nicolai shakes his head. "The queen will explain. Now get on."

Sasha casts a tight look at me, and then steps on to the sledge and seats herself at the front. I get aboard behind her, and Nicolai takes the reins, standing at the back. There's a jolt as the dogs take up the slack on the harness, and then we're through the gate and out into the forest, picking up speed.

Nicolai brings us around in an arc, and soon we're heading back towards the city, the wind burning cold on my cheeks. It's dark, but the dogs are sure-footed.

Nicolai says something, but I don't hear it the first time. He bends lower and says into my ear, "Any news of Feliks or Katia?"

I press my lips together and shake my head. I haven't seen them since the ceremony when we returned the stolen music box. They'd concealed themselves in the crowd, but I never got the chance to speak to them. "What about the pardons they were to receive? Do they still stand now?"

Nicolai doesn't answer.

Sasha shivers in front of me, and I tighten my arms around her. It stings that she didn't tell—*still* hasn't told—me everything she knows, but when I thought she was in danger again, something fierce rose up inside me and took over for a while.

The dogs are moving fast, and we approach the warehouse district, continuing past smaller houses to the wider streets of affluent areas, then the shops of the merchants' quarter, heading towards the square, the palace beyond cutting its clean lines into the night sky, pale and solid under a clear half-moon.

But Nicolai stops short of the square, guiding the dogs into the midst of the deserted marketplace. I stand slowly on stiff legs and hold my hand out to Sasha. She takes it, and we follow Nicolai past the snow-weighted awnings of empty stalls. All is silent.

When we reach the fountain in the middle of the square, Nicolai steps up on to it, beckoning us to follow. The water within is frozen, white and unmoving around the massive statue in the middle.

"I thought we were going to see the queen." I lift my chin towards the palace.

Nicolai glances around, though there's not a soul in the square, every shop shuttered and dark. "You are," he says in a low voice. He reaches out towards the huge back leg of the stone horse that rises from the fountain. There's a grating sound, and a doorway appears, with spiral steps leading down into the dark.

I turn to Sasha, but judging by the way her mouth hangs open, she had no idea this existed either. I knew there was a network of tunnels under the city—we used them to escape Tyur'ma. But it's still strange to find hidden places and secrets in a city I thought I knew.

I step forward, pressing one hand to the cold stone, and descend the steps, curling down and down beneath the fountain. Light bleeds up from the bottom of the staircase, dim at first, then growing brighter, until I step out into a large stone cavern. The air is old as crypts, the ceiling low and uneven. The walls are lined with braziers, torches burning orange and casting flickering shadows over the walls.

Queen Ana steps forward, wearing a simple dark gown, no *kokoshnik* on her head.

She looks straight at Nicolai. "How is he?"

"He is well, Your Majesty," says Nicolai. "All is secure. I knew you wished to see the Raisayevna sisters, so when I found them checking that Anatol was safe, I—"

"Both can speak for themselves, as we are all aware," says the queen, but not unkindly. "In the morning you will return to the house. Maintain your position; watch the other guards and report anything unusual to me and me alone."

Nicolai bows, and the queen nods. He turns and flits silently back up the stone stairs. My sister twists her hands together beside me. I think of another time I was brought before the queen—accused of trying to kill Prince Anatol, my mother pleading outside the throne-room doors—and shiver.

The queen raises an eyebrow. "How is it that you come to be in the exact place of my son's banishment, meant to be unknown to all, after midnight, Valor Raisayevna? I hope Sasha didn't—"

"You can't think Anatol had anything to do with Anastasia escaping," I blurt out.

Sasha's intake of breath at my outspokenness pulls me up short, but the queen is already shaking her head.

"No, Valor. I *know* my son is innocent. Perhaps I should explain, before I ask of you what I plan to ask." She steps closer, and the shadows release their hold on her. "After Anastasia's escape, and now with the rumours and accusations levelled at Anatol, I have no idea who I can trust." She gestures around us. "I cannot even meet with those I do trust without going to these lengths. Within the palace, who knows which eyes and ears remain loyal? Everywhere I hear whispers, but I do not believe that Anatol was in any way connected to Anastasia's plot to ally with Pyots'k.

"No one else seems to believe that, though. I had no choice but to publicly banish Anatol, but it is for his own safety as much as to show the people that they can still trust me. The people *must* place their trust in their queen. If I lose that, then I lose everything."

The queen paces the stone floor. Sasha's eyes are huge and dark. I know how she feels; my heart is beating strangely. I'm pinned in place by the force of what the queen is saying, the import of it.

"I trust your family," Queen Ana says abruptly. "I need your parents in my court. Your father and I must find out who is still loyal to me and who is not. We must know who helped Anastasia escape. But we must find out while keeping up our work on the peace process with Magadanskya. It's more important now than ever. Anastasia's plan to ally with Pyots'k may have failed, but Pyots'k still wants to use our ports to launch their warships, and our only hope of stopping them is if they're too afraid to invade Demidova because Magadanskya will join our side if they try."

She takes a breath and rubs her forehead. "How much has your father told you of the lands beyond the Sea of Mirn?"

I open my mouth, but then shake my head. I know very little.

"The land we call Saylas belongs to a dangerous, warlike people," says Sasha. "That's why it would be terrible for us to let Pyots'k launch their ships against them. If Pyots'k wages war and loses, the Saylish would follow them back here."

The queen nods. "We would be embroiled in a war in which we never wished to have any part. Between Saylas and Pyots'k, Demidova would become a battleground. The truth is that we have scant knowledge of Saylas, other than its reputation. We have never set sail there for a reason." Queen Ana frowns, and then says, more to herself, "Let us hope none of us ever have to."

She stops pacing directly in front of me. I stand tall, trying not to show the uncertainty I feel about why I'm being entrusted with this knowledge. The queen stands tall as well, looking directly into my eyes.

"Your father and I have much work to do to fend off Pyots'k, to make our relationship with Magadanskya strong enough that they will help us fight Pyots'k if we have to. This is *our* work.

"But you know my daughter. You know what she is capable of, and there is no one else I can trust right now. I wanted to see you because I have something to ask of you. Of both of you."

The queen turns to Sasha. "Prince Anatol had only just begun the work of overhauling our prison system. In his absence, and with your father so busy already, I would like you—under his supervision, of course—to continue the work. As someone who has been falsely accused and imprisoned in Tyur'ma, the people will trust you to do the job. Will you accept?"

My mind spins, chasing the idea of what the queen could want of me, but I can't fail to notice the flush of pleasure on Sasha's face. All her life she's wanted to follow Father, to become the queen's adviser when the time came.

We haven't talked about it, but I know how painful it was for her to think that such a path had been blocked to her when she was tossed into prison.

She bows. "It would be an honour, Your Grace."

The queen relaxes a fraction, but as she turns her attention back to me, I can almost see the weight on her shoulders. This past month, I've chafed under the fuss my mother has made over my sister and me. Now I think about how the queen must feel to have a daughter who's betrayed her. There's nothing I can say or do; I'm not the right person for this. Not old enough, not clever enough, not someone who can use words the way my father and sister do.

I swallow. "What will you ask of me, Queen Ana?"

She folds her hands to still them and squares her shoulders. "I am asking you to work for me, to answer to me alone. I am asking you to capture Anastasia."

The stifled rush of breath my sister lets out is the only sound in the chamber. I can't tear my gaze away from the queen.

"Valor, I must impress upon you that I can offer little in the way of assistance. I have issued a decree that Anastasia is to be brought to justice, but since she must have had help from within the palace, neither my court nor my Guard can as yet be trusted. I . . ." Her voice dips like a guttering candle. "Do you accept? Will you help me capture Anastasia and clear Anatol's name?"

I think about what the princess did to my sister, about how the ripples spread to my family, to Anastasia's own family, and through Demidova. And when I think about all she's done, about what *I'm* being asked to do, there's really nothing to think about at all.

"I do," I say. "I accept."

CHAPTER 4

When we step out into the fountain again, I almost expect something to have changed outside to match the dizzying blizzard in my head. Each piece of information I've learned tonight is a snowflake blowing in a multidirectional wind.

Instead, it's calm outside. The square is silent and quilted in perfect, untouched snow. It's still darkest night, though it feels as if it should be morning already.

Sasha and I don't talk as we trudge home, both of us turning over our new missions in our minds. When I drop into bed, I'm not sure what I'm going to do, but when I bolt upright a few short hours later, it's clear. Sasha and I leave the quiet house again before dawn, though it's not until we're nearing the square that either of us speaks.

"Where are you even going to start?" Sasha's voice cuts through the silence. The sun has begun to come up. I can't see it yet, but the light changes and the sky shifts. I breathe in the cold air and look out at the empty market. I know exactly what I need first.

"Feliks and Katia," I say. "They have something to tell me."

I saw them at the ceremony to hand the music box over to Lady Olegevna and make the treaty with Magadanskya official. I'm certain they came there to find me. I don't know for a fact that they do have anything to tell me, but the way I say it, with a little bit of emphasis on the word "they", is enough to make Sasha react.

"There's really nothing else I know that could help you at all, Valor. You have to understand that I couldn't just tell you about Anatol's banishment. And really, what would have been the point of worrying you when we were still in Magadanskya and there was nothing you could do about it? I would have told you when we got—"

"I know. I heard you the first time. It's going to be your job to keep secrets. Don't worry, I understand."

"Valor, don't be like that."

My boots crunch the ice as I step forward. I ran through this market with the entire Queen's Guard after me, threw part of my crossbow here, paused here—

"What are you doing now?" Sasha sounds tired. She looks it too, as she stops trudging and stares at me with dull eyes.

I almost feel bad as I duck down, dislodging snow as I heave off the cover of a market stall. As the snow falls, I see I'm right—this is the spot where Feliks was hiding on the day we both got arrested.

"Valor?"

I push underneath, squeezing into the spot where I hid before, and twist around, trying to hold up the cover so I can get some light. Sasha's face appears in the gap I've made. She's frowning, but she helps me hold the stiff canvas high.

A piece of paper is folded several times and wedged into a gap in the warped wood. My heart surges with triumph as I strip off my mitten to work the paper free. I know already that I'm right about who left it here—there's a smudgy fingerprint on it.

"Feliks," I say, and Sasha lets out a laugh.

I scramble out from under the stall and go to open the paper, but Sasha stills my hand. The sky is lightening rapidly, and a woman in dark furs appears across the square. The shutters on the bakery rattle open. In the distance, there's a metallic clatter.

I nod to my sister, and we move quickly away from the stall, through the market and out into a quiet street before I finally unfold the paper.

V,

Need to talk to you urgently.
Use the network.

F & K

Sasha reads upside down, her face close to mine. "What network?"

"I don't know." For a second, I'm blank. "No, wait—I do. Feliks told me about it. A thieves' network within the city."

Sasha looks around her as though she expects the network to be visible.

"They pass information, trade things on the black market . . ." I trail off, because I'm really not sure what they do. Or where to find them. But I need Feliks and Katia— and not just because they want to tell me something important enough to risk attending the ceremony before their pardons were finalised. I need to find them because I know how much harder it will be to do what Queen Ana's asked me to do on my own. I could never have got Sasha out of Tyur'ma without their help.

Around us, the market is coming to life. Snow is shifted off awnings, and bright fruit is laid out. A skinny figure slips between two stalls and I step forward, Feliks's name

right there in my mouth. But it's not him—not tall enough—
and the boy disappears into the growing mass of workers.

"The only thing I really know is that I met Feliks right
here at the market," I say.

Sasha half smiles. "Well then, it's a good thing I left a
note for Mother saying that we'd gone out early to come
here and get a proper Demidovan breakfast after all that
Magadanskyan palace food."

I feel a smile break across my face in spite of myself.
"In that case, I think we should stay right here and keep
our eyes open." My stomach growls. "I don't suppose you
brought any—"

Sasha pulls a purse from inside her furs and produces a
silver coin.

We have to wait another half hour, scouring the market
all the time for anyone who might be able to lead us to the
network, before we can order hot cocoa and sticky pastries.
Delicious steam wafts into the air in front of my face, but
the drink is still too hot. I've already scalded my tongue
while Sasha carefully blows across the top of her cup.

I look at the side of her face as she blows again, rippling
the surface of the liquid.

"It's cold today," she says.

"It's *always* cold."

"I really am sorry," she says quietly. "I barely knew
anything other than that Anatol was banished. You heard

what Queen Ana said—even the guard who came to tell us didn't know the truth of the matter. I bet not even Father does yet."

I cup my hands tighter around my cocoa. Leaving something out when you talk to someone is still lying. Across the market, a busker starts strumming a balalaika. Maybe she's getting an early start—I didn't think the festival started for days.

Sasha sighs. "I told you everything else the guard said, I really did. The only other news involved Princess Inessa coming to visit."

I search through my memories of the royal family for Inessa. "Which one is she?" I ask.

"She's Queen Ana's sister's second-eldest daughter, fourth in line for the throne. The family estate is—" Sasha stops and rolls her eyes at my expression. "She's the one who licked the icing on Anatol's birthday cake."

"Oh, her. What's she doing here?"

"It's a show of support from the family. The older sister is already doing diplomatic work with her mother in Magadanskya, so Inessa's going to attend functions with the queen in Anastasia's place."

I nod, but I can't muster up much pretence that I'm interested, the way I usually do when Sasha tells me what's going on at court. Instead we sink into silence. I begin to think that finding the letter from Feliks was more luck than judgement, but just as I'm trying to clean the last of the pastry glaze off my fingers to put my mittens back on, I catch a glimpse of someone familiar. Someone distinctive.

"Is that Mila?" I jut my chin in her direction, trying to be discreet, but the girl is limping straight for us through the growing crowd anyway. I'm so pleased to see her. She helped me back in Tyur'ma when no one else would. She saved my life before I'd even found Sasha's cell.

"It is," says Sasha. I hear eagerness in her voice. "Anatol must have pardoned her."

I can't help but wonder why not Feliks and Katia too, but after what Warden Kirov did to Mila, I'm glad it happened for her.

I take a step forward, but Mila walks right past us, saying in a low voice, "Follow me. I'll take you to them."

Sasha looks to me, and I nod. The snow crunches as we head into a side street. I hurry to keep up with Mila. Her gait is uneven, but she moves fast.

"Been waiting for you for quite a while," she says.

I move to walk at her side, the one with her good eye. "You were looking for me?"

"Katia and Feliks looked for you for days, until we found out you were in Magadanskya. Since then, they've been waiting for you to get back."

"I found their note," I say, unable to hide the hint of pride in my voice.

"Which one? They left those notes *everywhere* they thought you might look, and I've been out in the market-place watching for you the better part of every day."

"Oh."

Mila stops walking and nods. Ahead of us in the tiny, winding street is a narrow doorway I wouldn't have seen if it hadn't been open and Katia wasn't standing right there in it. Feliks is behind her, trying to peer over her shoulder and then, when that doesn't work, through the crook of her arm.

I hurry towards them. "Katia, I'm so happy to see you."

She returns my smile, but I know her; I can see the worry underneath her expression even when Feliks bursts out from behind her and flings a rough hug at my midsection.

We reach the door. Mila glances behind us as I peer inside to see a narrow, unlit hallway and a room where a fire blazes in a stone hearth.

"We weren't followed," Mila says to Feliks. Then, once Sasha and I step inside, Mila closes the door. I hear her boots crunch the snow as she walks away.

"Followed by who?" I ask. "Are you both all right? I saw you that day at the ceremony. But you're going to be par-doned. Why haven't you just come forward? Prince Anatol wou—"

"Prince Anatol's been banished," says Feliks. "Come on, let's talk in here. We've got a lot to tell you."

Katia squeezes my arm briefly, and I follow her and Sasha into the room. Feliks stokes the fire, and a damp, woody smell fills the space. There isn't any furniture, just some rugs on the floor, so we sit on them, and I place my crossbow at my side.

"What is it?" I ask.

Katia and Feliks look at each other. Katia's sandy hair, twisted into braids, slips over one shoulder. "The day of the escape," she says, "after we got out of the tunnel and on to the dock, we heard Natalia trying to get Sasha to go with her."

"Something was up," says Feliks. "Why would she want Sasha to go with her? If you'd seen the look on her face, how desperate she was, you'd have thought it was strange too."

"So we knew we had to follow her," Katia cuts back in. She frowns at a smudge of soot that's found its way on to Feliks's eyebrow. "It was clear she was up to something."

"She was—working for Princess Anastasia," says Sasha, a note of bitterness in her voice.

Feliks leans forward, nodding. "Natalia met the princess herself down by the docks. She wore a cloak with the hood pulled low, but I knew it was her. So I crept closer—close enough to see a purse change hands. She raised her voice too when she heard what had happened—that you and Sasha never got out of the tunnel. Stamped her foot and threw a proper fit. Vowed she'd make both of you and her brother suffer."

Sasha's head snaps up.

Feliks crosses his arms. "I know. Look what she already did to Prince Anatol. That's why we've been dying to speak to you all this time." He shakes his head. "Anyway, that's when the princess handed over the money to Natalia, and Natalia asked what they were going to do next, and . . ."

"And what?" I ask. "What's she going to do next?"

Feliks's big teeth bite into his lower lip. "Don't know. She stopped shouting then, so I couldn't hear that part. And I couldn't get any closer without getting caught."

I clamp my hands on my knees. My damp trousers are starting to dry, the fire's warmth seeping through to my legs. The flames pop and spit. "You should have told the queen," I say. "She could have . . ." But I trail off. What could she have done?

"What?" asks Katia, a challenge in her eyes. "You've been in a *palace* this past month, Valor. We've been in hiding, frightened to go anywhere. At least in Tyur'ma we knew where we stood."

"She's right," says Feliks. "Do you think the thieves' network would have let us back into places like this if we showed our faces to the queen? We couldn't take the chance. She might never have pardoned us. She might have sent us back to Tyur'ma."

I can feel Sasha looking at me. I take a deep breath. "So . . . how would you two feel if I said the queen just this morning charged me with finding Anastasia? And that I wanted to ask you to help me do it?"

Katia huffs in frustration. "What? No, Valor. Didn't you hear what Feliks just said?" She shakes her head. "We didn't tell you this so you would try to stop her. We wanted to warn you so you and Sasha could stay safe. What do you think Anastasia wants to do to you? What do you think she'd do to the likes of us?"

"That's exactly why I have to stop her," I say. "What you've told me only makes it more important that I do."

Katia just presses her lips together and worries the end of her braid.

I turn so the sides of my damp boots face the fire. I'll do this without them if I have to, but it surprises me how much I really *want* their help.

I stare into the flames. "Right now, Natalia's my best lead. She's the only one who knows anything about where the princess is. I have to go to the docks."

Feliks makes a noise somewhere between a grumble and a snort.

"What?" I ask.

"There's no saying Natalia's even still there. Plus there's every chance thieves, pirates and press gangs are. It's not all pretty sailing boats down there, you know. The people getting aboard some of those ships are desperate for one reason or another—and trust me, none of the reasons are good." Feliks scrutinises me. "I'm not even close to convincing you not to do this, am I?"

"I *have* to, Feliks. What's the alternative? Let Anastasia get away with what she already did to my family? Let her do something worse? And what about Anatol? After everything he did for Sasha and me, I can't just abandon him. Besides, I can't ignore what the queen herself has asked me to do. Sasha and I both have work to do for her."

Sasha nods. "I'm to take over Anatol's work at Tyur'ma."

Feliks sits bolt upright. "You can pardon us?"

Sasha's face falls.

"Only the queen can do that," says Katia quietly.

Feliks opens his mouth at that last part, but one look at Sasha has him closing it again. He still looks like he's bitten orange peel at any mention of the queen, though.

I'm uncomfortable sitting on the floor, too warm from the fire in front of me and too cold from the draught blowing on my back. I feel the same way inside. Katia and Feliks could have got their pardons while Anatol was free, but they didn't come forward just to keep their links with the thieves' network, just so they could wait out here to tell me what they knew about Natalia. Now their chance at getting pardons is gone. This isn't how I pictured seeing Katia and Feliks again now that we're all out of Tyur'ma.

Katia rests her chin on her knees and stares into the fire. I want to say something, but I know from sharing a cell with her that it's better if I don't.

Feliks's eyes dart from me to Katia to Sasha.

I hold out as long as I can, but patience isn't my strong suit. "Oh, saints. Somebody say something." I get to my feet and strap my crossbow back into place. "I'm going to the docks."

When I get to the door and turn around, the other three are standing too. Feliks pulls his furs into place.

I shake my head. "I thought—"

Katia marches past me. "Feliks and I need those pardons, and with Anatol banished, we need to get them from the queen."

Feliks follows her. "She's right. I'm not happy about it, Valor, but if the queen needs Anastasia found, then so do we."

CHAPTER 5

"Sasha," I say as Feliks peeks out through the front door. I hesitate, biting the corner of my lip. I don't know how I'm going to say what I need to say.

She raises her eyebrows.

"I think maybe you should—I mean, you could . . . instead of . . ."

The coast is clear, and Feliks ushers us all back outside.

"What?" Sasha asks.

I don't want her coming with us. There's something not quite right between us still, but I can't bear the thought of her doing something dangerous. Seeing her caught by Nicolai at the house made me realise I can't do it. Not after she just got out of Tyur'ma. Not after I just got her back. I can't lose her again.

I look at the ground and scuff my boot in the snow. "It's already way after breakfast. If one of us doesn't go back, Mother and Father will worry."

"You don't want me to come?" There's an edge of hurt in her voice, and I raise my eyes to hers.

"It's not that." But it is, a little.

She opens her mouth to protest, but then understanding flashes in her eyes. She blinks. "You're right. I can't do as the queen asked and help Father reform Tyur'ma if I'm chasing escaped criminals through the streets."

"Technically, *we're* escaped criminals," says Feliks with a grin that reminds me of when I first met him. Katia rubs the cuff of her fur over the sooty mark on his face, but it only fades to grey.

Sasha takes my hand. "I'll tell Mother . . . Well, I'll tell her something that doesn't involve the docks." She drops her coin purse into my palm. "Just in case."

I squeeze her hand, then slip the purse into my pocket and pull my mittens on. "I'll see you soon."

Feliks knows a way through the backstreets that he insists we take. Though they're still piled high with snow, not clear like the main streets, I'm glad he does. I feel wary and unsettled, and I'm glad to be on lesser-known paths.

The sun is up in the sky, iced lemon against pale blue. Narrow houses lean over us on both sides of the street. The way Feliks and Katia keep checking around us puts me on edge. But I need to be on edge. The princess had eyes and ears inside the prison—she could have them anywhere.

Feliks glances up. "Good thing we found each other early today. Much better to be at the docks in the light of day."

I smell the docks before I see them—a briny tinge of salt water, wet wood and fish carrying on the air. Before long, Feliks's route leads us out of a tiny alley and on to the dockside. Far around the curve of the harbour, a small fleet of great sailing ships sits on the water, some with sails furled tight, others with them hanging from their masts.

"Watch it."

I'm shoved backwards, my bow scraping against the wall of the pawnshop we've just passed. A hulking figure scowls at me and then stomps past, her boots grinding into the dirty, snow-covered cobbles.

"Heads down," says Feliks. "Don't draw attention. Just let me ask around. I'll find out if anyone knows where Natalia might be."

He darts away, leaping over a plank that joins the dockside to a tar-covered wreck of a ship that looks as though it's held together more by barnacles and grim determination than any carpentry skills. Sailors wheel goods up and down the plank, cursing at one another as they shift stinking crates of fish.

A bell jangles behind us, and Katia leaps forward as the door of the pawnshop is flung open and a woman with a filthy scarlet tunic showing beneath her furs bangs out through it. I pull Katia out of the way and into the mouth of the alley. She peeks around the corner, and I watch her wary face as she scans the scene. It makes me smile, remembering the night Warden Kirov shoved me into Katia's cell right after I arrived at Tyur'ma. After that first conversation, I never thought she'd help me, much less become my friend.

My smile fades. Katia's fingers, pressed against the stone wall, are even thinner than before. I have to make sure she gets pardoned.

I shift my weight back and forth between my feet. "How long do you think Feliks is going to be?"

Katia shakes her head, her eyes still on the sailors. "You're dealing with thieves and sailors, so who knows? Took us an entire day to find out where you'd gone and when you were coming back. The queen didn't exactly advertise your trip to Magadanskya."

I never even thought about it that way. I was desperate to get back to Katia and Feliks and find out what they wanted to tell me, but it hadn't occurred to me that they wouldn't know where I was. They must have been just as worried as I was, and they could have left the city at any time.

I touch Katia's arm. "Thanks for sticking around. For . . . for everything," I tell her.

She focuses her attention on me for a second and smiles. "It was the right thing to do," she says. Her smile fades too. "You were right. What you said back at the house? I might not like it, but it's still true: we have to find the princess. We'll never really be free if we don't."

She goes back to her watch, so I do too. Just down from the pawnshop a door keeps banging open and shut. When it's open, music and loud voices spill out from within. A tavern. I've never been in one, but after some time watching, it seems that every other person who crosses the docks also crosses the doorway of the tavern. And after some more watching, with no sign of Feliks, I'm even more convinced of what I need to do.

"Keep watch for Feliks. I'll be back in a minute," I say. Before Katia can answer, I step out of the alley and dodge my way through the busy street. The tavern door swings open. I duck in, and the door closes behind me.

A sickly sweet smell hits me, along with a dense cloud of smoke. I blink at the gloomy interior, and a few patrons look at me curiously.

My heart beats hard, but I step up to the bar at the back of the room as though I know what I'm doing and lean on the wooden counter.

"What are you doing in here, girl?" calls a rough voice from behind me.

I don't turn around, just focus on the bar in front of me.

The woman behind it splays her big hands on the shiny lacquered surface and jerks her chin at me by way of asking what I want. I can tell by her frown that I have about three seconds before she slings me out.

"I'm looking for somebody," I say quickly. "A girl named Natalia—"

"Lot of people looking for a lot of other people around here." The woman's frown deepens. "What makes you think anyone's going to tell you anything about somebody else's business? In fact, what do you think you're doing coming in here in the first place?"

Several pairs of eyes are on me now, and the smoke in the air—or something else—is making me itch under my furs. It might be the sweat breaking out on my skin. I lift my arm up from the bar, and my sleeve sticks before it pulls free. Maybe this wasn't one of my better ideas.

I cast a glance over my shoulder and turn around fast. I've taken three steps back towards the door before I even know it.

I burst out into the street just as someone calls out at me. The door cuts off something very unsavoury, and I dash back to Katia, whose lips are pursed so tightly that I can barely see them.

Feliks is back with her. "What were you thinking going in there?" he asks. "Valor, I know you did a great job getting us out of Tyur'ma, but you're not invincible. Even Warden Kirov had rules, but things aren't like that out here." He pulls out two small coins and rubs them together between his finger and thumb. "This is what talks out here. So I hope you've got some, because I just made a big promise to a girl in the network, and you're going to have to make good on it."

I start to pull out the purse Sasha gave me, but Feliks pushes it back into my pocket. "Not here!"

I swallow. "Sorry."

"Just follow me," he says. There's a hint of impatience in his voice, and I deserve it. He's right—I'm just as out of place here as I was in Tyur'ma, but he's still wearing the same patched furs he had on when I first met him.

I keep my mouth shut and my eyes cast down, following Feliks as he winds between dockworkers and sailors, travellers shrouded in heavy cloaks and vendors hawking their wares. The dirty snow beneath my boots is stained pink in patches. I step around them, and Katia nudges me. Feliks has stopped by a tiny girl with a tray of fire inch-sticks hanging around her neck.

"This her?" she says to Feliks. He nods, and the girl glances around and holds out a small, grimy hand. I pull out my purse halfway, then look to Feliks. He nods, so I take out a silver coin and place it on the girl's palm. Her fingers curl around it and it disappears before I even realise her hand has moved.

"I know Natalia," she says. "But she's actually been pretty nice to me. What do you want her for?"

My heart picks up its pace. "I only want to talk to her," I say. "Just ask a few questions, that's all."

The girl glances away from us, then back. "Maybe I can pass on a message," she says, holding out her hand again.

My fingers tighten around the purse. "I really need to talk to her myself. Do you know where she is, or don't you?"

She glances away again, but this time she shakes her head, just the tiniest movement.

I follow her gaze to a squat building to our left. Through the smeared glass of a window someone stares straight at me. Her eyes widen. Natalia.

The girl in front of me flings down her tray and snatches my purse, ripping it out of my hand. She dashes away, quick as a rat, paying no attention to Katia's outraged cry.

Feliks says something behind me, but I'm already running towards Natalia. I swing the door open. A blast of rancid air hits me, and then I'm spinning to the left and running flat-out. Natalia sprints ahead of me, out another door and back on to the docks, weaving through the passengers, sailors and tradespeople all churning the snow on the cobbles into a grey slush.

Natalia runs straight up the plank on to the ship I noticed earlier, pushing past a sailor trundling a crate on a wheelbarrow. I follow, my feet bouncing with the slight give of the plank under my boots. There's a shout and a hand grabs for me, but its fingers only graze my crossbow and then slip away.

I leap on to the ship, but Natalia's fast—or desperate. She crosses the deck and darts behind a stack of crates, and

I lose sight of her. I push harder, out of breath. My boots slide under me on the damp wood. My heartbeat kicks up another level as I slip, but I right myself, dodging around the crates just in time to see Natalia land and roll on the deck of another ship.

I scramble over to the side of the ship just as the one Natalia jumped on to moves sideways, cracking the thin sheet of ice across the surface of the sea below. She looks back at me, and a smile starts to curl on her face. I launch myself at the deck she's on. As soon as I do, I know that I've miscalculated. I'm going to come up short.

Panic bursts through me as I lunge forward, reaching for the side of the ship. My mittens make contact just before my body slams into the curved planks of the hull. It knocks the breath out of me. My face presses against the salt-soaked wood. If I hang here for long, I'll lose my grip and plunge straight into the freezing water below.

I pull as hard as I can and try to find purchase with my feet, but my boots can't get any traction. My breath huffs out. I look down. The water is grey beneath the cracked panes of ice. The gap between the boats is narrowing again. If they meet, I'll be crushed.

My right hand slips out of my mitten and I shout, swinging my arm back up, grabbing at the edge. I look back. The ship is closer. Then someone grabs my arm from above and hauls me upwards, my shoulder almost wrenching apart.

I'm dragged over the edge and hit the deck with a thump. I look up to thank my rescuer, but the face above me isn't concerned, it's scowling, thick eyebrows pulled low, and there's a hand reaching for my bow. I jump up and run, pushing past three other sailors in oilskins who are heading my way. The end of the plank that leads back on to the dock thumps, and I see Natalia running full tilt towards an alley.

I follow, my shoulder burning every time I pump my arm. I'm not losing her now. She wouldn't be running unless she had something to hide. I hit the cobbles, stumble forward and then take off again, trying to keep up. Natalia swings around, and I dodge behind an overflowing barrel at the mouth of the alley. The stink of fish emanates from the wooden slats I press against.

I peer around the curve of the barrel. Natalia's still standing there, breathing hard, scanning the people walking the docks. I wait, hoping she doesn't bolt again. Her shoulders relax and she turns, casting a final glance over her shoulder before she hurries away.

But she's no longer running.

I slip out from behind the barrel and trail her, hanging back a little. She moves fast, throwing furtive glances behind her every now and then, winding through the alleys that twist alongside the docks. We pass taverns that are smaller and dingier than the one on the dockside and several buildings proclaiming they have rooms available. I've never seen these parts of Demidova before, but I don't have time to wonder about them now. I keep my eyes on Natalia's broad back until she stops, looks both ways, and then slips into a narrow doorway. My heart is still beating fast from the chase, but it steps up further now. She thinks she's lost me, so where is she going?

I slip out from the cover of a water trough and run up to the doorway. A startled cat bolts out, and I suck in a breath. But I step over the threshold and into a thin corridor, dark and smelling vaguely like the tavern, with a series of closed doors stretching the length of it. A scuffle behind one sends my gaze darting to it.

I reach back and pull my crossbow into my hands. Not exactly the ideal weapon for an enclosed space, but much better than nothing. I step forward. The door's slightly ajar, and more noise comes from the room beyond—boots hurrying over a stone floor.

I look through the crack. Natalia crouches on the floor. A satchel lies next to her, its flap open and spilling clothes that have been hastily shoved inside. She's messing with something in front of her, but I can't see what. I nudge the door with the tip of my bolt, but it creaks. Natalia jumps back, and then springs to her feet. I clutch my crossbow tight and kick the door wide, levelling my weapon at her.

She glances at a small grimy window behind her.

"I wouldn't even think about it if I were you," I say. I can feel my heart beating in the fingertips that are taut on my crossbow.

"What do you want, Valor?" Natalia narrows her eyes, trying for a nonchalant attitude, but she's backed up against a wooden chair behind her, her hands clasping it.

"Where's Anastasia?" I ask.

Natalia lets out a humourless laugh. "I'll tell you where she's not. She's not here."

I take a step farther into the room and tighten my finger over the trigger. Natalia swallows.

"Where is Anastasia?"

"Just stop. I wouldn't tell you that even if I did know." Her eyes dart towards a chest of drawers—the only piece of furniture in the room apart from the chair and a low pallet bed—and then back to me. "Look where we are, Valor. Do you really think I know where the princess is just because she once paid me to do something for her? I don't know anything."

I can't tell whether she's lying or not, but I switch tack anyway. "OK. But you know what she's planning. What is it? What else has she paid you to do? *Who* else has she paid?"

Natalia's mouth twists into a smile. "The princess does like her revenge." A sly look crosses her face. "But that's not all she wants. Let me go and I'll tell you that much."

I shake my head. "You're not in a position to bargain. Tell me and I might not release this bolt."

She looks at the tip of my crossbow. I can see that she's angry and scared and squirming like a worm on a hook. I don't try to hide my satisfaction.

Natalia swallows again. She's trapped, and she knows it.

"Why did she have Prince Anatol banished?" I ask. "What's she up to?"

"Do you think I'm privy to all her plans?" Natalia blurts out. "I have no idea where she is or what she's going to do next. Look at me, hiding in this hole."

"You know something," I say. "What do you think she wants?"

Natalia shrugs—a quick, irritated motion. "She wants what she's always wanted—the throne. Did you think she was going to stop just because her mother said she can never have it now? She only wants it more. And when Anastasia wants something . . ."

I'm fully aware of the lengths the princess will go to. My whole family is painfully aware. I think about my sister, huddled on the floor of a solitary cell among the Black Hands at Tyur'ma. About my mother crying in the night after they'd taken Sasha.

Footsteps echo in the hallway. I'm distracted for only an instant, but Natalia dashes forward with a cry. I turn to keep my crossbow trained on her, but it's Feliks I see. He's right outside the door. She barrels straight into him, knocking him back into Katia. I lurch forward, dropping my bow and reaching out to grab Natalia. My fingers close around her satchel strap and the buckle gives, but Natalia is gone, leaving Feliks and Katia on the floor and me clutching nothing but the satchel itself.

"How did you find me?" I ask.

"You made quite a show on the docks," says Feliks sourly. "After that we just followed you." Katia pushes Feliks off her legs, and they both scramble up to go after Natalia.

"Wait!" I say. "We need to search this place."

"You do it. I'll go after her." Katia darts away. Feliks looks between the two of us and then bolts after Katia.

I hesitate. Most of me wants to go with them, but if I leave now, I might not have the chance to get in here again. Natalia could come back here before I find out what she was looking at.

I go straight to the chest of drawers.

The wood is warped, and I have to jiggle the top drawer out of its frame. It's empty. I try the next drawer, and the last—all empty. I upend the pallet bed.

I hear steps outside and dart behind the door.

"It's us," calls Feliks. "We lost her." He steps into the room. "Next time you go dashing off like that, you might consider taking me with you." He's still out of breath. "I bet you barely know where you are."

"Sorry," I say. "The opportunity was there. I had to take it."

"What did she tell you?" asks Katia. Her cheeks are still pink from running.

"Everything she knows, I *think*," I say. "But she kept looking over there." I gesture, but there's barely anything to gesture at.

Katia surveys the open drawers and the bed. "There's nothing here," she says. "We should all have gone after her."

Maybe Katia's right. "I just really thought she was hiding something."

Feliks runs his fingers over the tops of the door frame and the window, then turns back to me and shakes his head.

Katia's right. There's nothing here. Natalia's never going to come back here. We'll never find her again. My gaze lands on the satchel.

She was packing.

In a hurry.

I snatch up the bag and tip it out on to the floor. The rough material of a few spare clothes falls out, along with a small notebook. Feliks makes a noise of surprise, and both he and Katia step in close as I stand and open the book.

"What is it?" he asks, looking from me to Katia and back again. I flip through the tiny pages. There are dates and times, and each of them has a brief note next to it, some including an amount of money.

"I think these are details of everything she did for the princess." I pause on a page that says "Tower fire", then on another that says "Docks".

Feliks frowns. "Are you sure? Why would she write them down?"

We're all quiet for a moment.

"Maybe . . . as a kind of insurance policy?" says Katia.

"Yes. Proof of what she'd been asked to do," I say. "Just in case she ever needed it."

Feliks's eyes are wide, and I'm hoping it's not with admiration. "To blackmail the princess?" he asks.

I shrug. "Maybe. Or in case she ever got caught—to prove that she was acting on orders."

"Clever," says Feliks. "I mean, terrible, of course," he adds hastily, "but you have to admit, it's clever too."

I riffle through the pages until I find the last entry. Katia and I read the date and time and look up at each other.

"What? *What?*" Feliks shakes my arm. His fingers are filthy with dust from the door frame.

"This is today's date," I say.

Katia squints out of the window, up at the sun. "In about three hours' time."

"Well, what's *happening*?" Feliks almost shouts.

I flip the pages back and forth, just to make sure. "It doesn't say. All it says is 'Queen Ana'."

Katia touches the notebook. "You need to get this to her."

I nod. "And tell her what little Natalia told me about Anastasia. She still intends to rule Demidova."

"Valor?" The look on Feliks's face as he stares past us makes me turn around fast. Standing in the doorway is one of the huge sailors from the ship I ran across, and behind her I count three more. The smell of the sea and the tavern rolls off them, sour and wild. A length of chain wrapped around the woman's fist rattles out of her hand, and one end hits the floor.

CHAPTER 6

I instantly look to my crossbow, still lying on the floor where I dropped it when I grabbed for Natalia. The woman takes one swift step into the room and kicks the bow behind her. The chain she's wielding drags along the floor with a solid iron slither that sets my teeth on edge. Feliks clutches my arm.

"We'll be on our way," says Katia. Her tone is hard, but I hear the edge of fear in it.

"I don't think so," says the woman. She has pale skin and an accent like Katia's. Her hair hangs in matted braids shot through with beads. Feliks sidles away from me. We glance at each other, and I understand: he wants us to spread out and try to get away. He's right. I won't stop him the way I did when Peacekeeper Rurik came to collect us from the palace.

But with the woman in front of us, the four of us take up most of the space in the cramped room. Another sailor blocks the doorway. I'm completely on edge, aware of everything; I see all the dirt in his beard, the broken leather lace on his tunic.

Feliks dodges right, Katia breaks left, and I do the only thing I can: run straight at the woman, sidestepping and twisting past her. Fingers swipe the air by my arm, and my heart is hammering—and then suddenly, abruptly, I'm yanked to a stop, pinned in front and back by two sailors who are each a full head taller than I am.

I open my mouth to shout. Someone grabs my arms from behind, and a sack is pulled over my head, muffling the sound I let out. I thrash around and yell, but the cloth is pulled tight, and I cough. It stinks of fish. Next to me I hear Feliks shouting out, and then a thump followed by a muffled cry.

My eyes are wide against the sudden darkness inside the sack, and the reek of fish clings to the back of my throat. My arms are held taut at an uncomfortable angle as someone shoves me forward. I stumble, but my captor catches me roughly and pushes me onwards. We march along the corridor and then out into the cold air. My boots tread snow. I'm jostled by a shorter person to my left.

"Feliks?"

Someone cuffs me on the side of the head, and the sudden blow sets my ear ringing. Now it's harder to tell where I am and where anyone else is. The only thing I know is that we're surrounded and being herded, saints know where, by four strangers who definitely don't wish us well. I shake my head, trying to clear the buzzing. My ear is hot and throbs in time with my heartbeat.

My arms begin to hurt from being pulled up behind my back every time I slow or stumble. I try to keep track of the twists and turns as we walk, but it becomes impossible, and all I can think about is my own warm breath heating the filthy sack over my face and filling my lungs with the reek of rotting fish.

Eventually I hear voices, and the call of seabirds becomes more insistent. The cobbles feel slushy under my feet, and then I trip over a step and get hauled up again on to a narrow board that bows beneath my feet. I recognise it instantly from chasing Natalia—a gangplank. Someone grabs the front of my tunic and hurls me down on to slippery wood. I'm on the deck of a ship; I can feel the rocking motion. There are two thuds beside me, and Katia shouts but is cut off as though her voice just vanished.

I hear a bang that vibrates through the wood where I lie struggling to right myself with my hands held behind my back, and then I'm dragged backwards by the collar of my furs. The floor drops out from under me. I cry out as I fall and then hit something solid, knocking all my breath out of me.

Two more heavy thuds sound beside me, and then above me something slams. I lie breathless for a few seconds, waiting for everything that hurts to stop hurting.

"Valor?"

It's Feliks, sounding shaky.

"I'm here. I'm all right," I say, though my heart is still beating wildly and my arms are burning. "Katia?"

"Here too. Are we on a ship?"

"I think so," I say. Above us are muffled sounds of boots and other heavier bangs. I wriggle my way upright and drop my head between my knees, shaking it in order to get the sack off. I have to wedge the end of the material between my boots to pull it off. I blink at Katia, who's already managed to get the sack off her head. Her braids have pulled free in places, and there's a cut on her lip, the blood already crusted.

Feliks shakes free of his sack like a dog. We're in a dim room filled with wooden barrels and burlap sacks. The walls are solid planks of wood, and there's a heavy hatch above us—the one we must have been thrown through.

"What do they want with us?" I ask.

Feliks sighs, twisting into a position that allows him to rest his back against a small ironbound keg. "To sell us? To work the ship until we drop from exhaustion and then toss us overboard? Who knows. I told you the docks weren't a place we wanted to come," he says. "And they're definitely not a place to draw attention to yourself."

My skin prickles even though the air is close and dank. "I'm sorry. I never meant for anything like this to happen."

"We should have waited, not rushed into anything," says Katia. "We should have had a better plan. Now all we've got is some notebook that proves nothing, and look where we are."

I'd almost forgotten about the notebook. The date and time—two o'clock this afternoon. And next to that, the queen's name.

Panic hits me. "I dropped the notebook. We have nothing to show the queen." I struggle forward, a fresh sense of fear rushing through me.

Feliks's face is creased in concentration. He's trying to work free of his bonds using the iron nails in the keg.

"What time do you think it is?" I ask.

Katia shakes her head. Her eyes are bright with fear, like those of a hunted animal. "Valor, you're not listening. *Look where we are.* Who cares whether you have anything to show the queen if she never sees you again?"

She's right. I manage to get to my knees. The ship pitches and throws me off balance.

Feliks huffs in frustration; his keg has tipped over and he's lost purchase on the nail he was using. Black powder spills out of the barrel on to the floor.

"Katia, come here," I say. "Turn around." I back up to her and reach out for her wrists. "Feliks, if you stand and watch, you can tell me what I need to do to loosen these knots."

He nods and tells me where to find the ends of the rope that binds Katia's hands. I work at the knots until my fingers are numb and bruised, and finally they start to give.

"That's it. They're coming apart," he says.

Katia starts twisting her wrists back and forth, loosening the ropes more and more until she gives a little cry, and I spin around to see her rubbing her hands, her wrists red and chafed in places.

She flexes her fingers, glances at the hatch, and then starts tugging and pulling at my rope. I can't wait to get it off.

It doesn't take long before my arms spring apart and I can finally move my sore shoulders. While Katia unties Feliks, I drag a barrel to the centre of the room. Then we set a crate on top of the barrel. I clamber up, hoping the sea beneath us doesn't decide to fling a wave at the ship, and then stretch to reach the hatch.

I push it, gingerly at first—anyone could be up above. When the hatch doesn't move, I push harder, then again as hard as I can. It doesn't budge even a fraction.

"Look around for something we can use for leverage," I say.

Feliks starts scrambling around the room, lifting sacks that release clouds of black dust. I wait impatiently, still trying to force the hatch or at least to peer through the cracks in the wood above me.

"It's nothing but barrels and sacks and *this*," says Feliks, shoving a rusty old cannon, which doesn't move at all. "Katia? Anything?"

Katia pushes her damp hair back from her face and shakes her head. "Nothing. But let me try the hatch. I'm taller than you are, Valor."

I jump down and Katia takes my place, heaving at the hatch while I take a turn searching the room, tearing aside sacking, kicking our discarded ropes across the floor. The more I search, the more I realise there's nothing here that can help us. The sounds of the dock are so faint that they barely carry down here. No one would hear us shouting. No one would care.

There's a sudden lurch, followed by muffled shouts from way above us. The ship rocks, and a great clanking sound fills the space. It's almost like . . . the cell doors in Tyur'ma rolling back. When I pause, trying to force myself to think, I notice Katia. She's on the floor with her back to the barrel we dragged beneath the hatch, hugging her knees to her chest.

"Katia?"

She stares straight ahead, her eyes dull, and suddenly I'm back at the prison meeting my cellmate for the first time. She was huddled on her bunk then, her back to me. I thought she was rude and fussy. I thought she didn't care. I still don't know how long she'd been locked in that cell before I arrived; she won't tell me.

I run over to her and drop to my knees. "I'll get you out of here, I promise."

"I wanted to go home, to the village, to the blue mountains," she says, her voice so faint that I can barely hear it. "I wanted to see Pyots'k again."

Katia's head drops to her knees, and she wraps her arms around her legs, her hands clasping her wrists so tightly they go white. I put my arms around her until the noise stops. The ship sways and pitches.

"Was that what I think it was?" asks Feliks in a tight voice. He's standing with his feet apart to keep his balance. "It sounded like an awful lot of chain."

"They've pulled the anchor up," I say. "The ship is heading out to sea."

Katia lets out a whimper, and I shiver. When I was stuck in the ice dome at Tyur'ma, she didn't hesitate to smash the ice to get me out. When we were running from the warden in the tunnels under the prison, she never stopped.

I've never seen her this scared.

"We have to get out of here before there's nowhere for us to go," I say. I don't want to leave Katia's side, but I have to do something. I stand up fast and look around again.

I start shoving at the sacks. All I see is the hull of the ship. I roll a small barrel out of the way, and then twist a heavier one on its base to move it aside. More solid hull. The ship rocks again, and Katia stifles a sob. I can't bear to see her like this.

Feliks helps me move a crate with a couple of rusty iron balls in it, and my heart leaps. "Look at this!" There's a battened-down opening in the wood: a square just big enough for us to squeeze through. "If we can get it open . . ." There are hinges on the top of it, like a big flap in the side of the boat.

Feliks and I both shove. It's rusted shut. I'm getting desperate. Feliks keeps trying, pushing his thin shoulder into the wood, his feet sliding across the planks of the floor.

"The cannon!" I say.

He stops, out of breath. "As a battering ram?" he asks. "It's too heavy. We won't be able to move it."

"Then let's use it," I say. "Blast a hole in the side."

His eyes widen, his gaze flying to the barrel of black powder he knocked over. "Gunpowder?"

I nod. "And cannonballs."

"I don't know, Valor. It looks really old. It probably doesn't work. It could be dangerous."

I try to smile, even though I know he's right. "Where's the Feliks who tried to run from a Peacekeeper?" I ask him.

"OK, Valor," he says. "But if I lose fingers, I'll want more than a pardon from Queen Ana. How do we even do this?"

"I've read about it," I say. Mother's book collection is tiny compared to Father's, but it covers all manner of weapons—my mother is proficient with more than just the bow and knife.

I rip apart a piece of sacking and tell Feliks to scoop up the spilled gunpowder and wrap it tightly. While he's doing that, I lift one of the cannonballs out of the crate and roll the other two around. There's only one fuse, lying forgotten among strands of straw.

"Feliks? Please tell me you have a fire inch-stick."

There's a pause. I turn around, panic clawing at me again.

Feliks is holding up two sticks. "Never go anywhere without them—not since . . . you know," he says.

I let out a breath. It was dark in the tunnels under the prison, and we might never have found our way out if Sasha hadn't found the lamps and fire inch-sticks.

"Pack it in tight," I say, pointing to the muzzle of the cannon. Feliks feeds the parcel of powder in, and I follow it with a cannonball that leaves flakes of rusted iron all over my hands.

We have nothing to pack the ball and powder down with, and I have no idea if the cannon will even work, but this is our only chance, so I try not to think about it. I push the fuse into the barrel until it meets the powder, and give Feliks a nod.

I glance at Katia, but she hasn't moved. "You will see Pyots'k again," I tell her, though I don't know if she can hear me.

Feliks strikes the fire inch-stick and holds it to the fuse. It doesn't light. The stick burns down until Feliks gasps and drops it to the floor. We both stare at the last inch-stick, and Feliks shakes his head. He doesn't have any more.

"We have the worst luck." He jerks his head upwards. "How did this bunch even find us?"

I freeze.

"What?" asks Feliks.

"Maybe it had nothing to do with luck," I say. "Maybe they found us because they knew where Natalia lived. And if they knew where Natalia lived, then it's because—"

"They work for Princess Anastasia!" Feliks's mouth turns down. "Here." He holds the inch-stick out to me. "You do it, Valor."

I take the stick from him and light it carefully, all my focus on the tiny flame at the end. I hold my breath and move my hand slowly, so slowly, over to the fuse.

It sparks to life with a fizz.

"Move back!" I pull Feliks over to where Katia still sits, and we all crouch behind the big barrel. I cover my ears, and Feliks does the same. It takes forever for the fuse to burn down.

I lift my hands away from my ears a little, certain the flame has gone out.

There's a deep echoing bang that I feel inside my chest, and acrid smoke fills the space. My ears ring, and I blink and cough. But I jump to my feet, clasping Katia's hand and pulling her with me.

Feliks barges into me, coughing. "Did it work?" he asks.

I wave my free hand, trying to clear the smoke. Shouts sound above us.

"Come on!" I run forward. Splintered wood surrounds a jagged hole in the side of the ship, and through it I can see the dock.

And the expanse of sea between us and it.

But there's no time to think about that. "Jump," I say to Feliks. "It's not that far. We can make it. Hurry."

Feliks scrambles up to the hole and launches himself out without a backwards glance.

Katia pulls back on my hand, mumbling something. Below us, there's a splash.

"What?" I try to tug her forward again.

"I can't swim," she says.

And suddenly I remember Katia telling me about her sister who drowned. She's blamed herself since it happened. She tried so hard to do the right thing, to earn her pardon. And now she's faced with this? I can't even imagine how scared she must be.

"Oh, Katia. I'm so sorry." I take both her hands in mine and look out at the grey sea. Feliks is surging through the water like a fish, his thin arms slicing the waves. "I won't leave you."

The hatch opens, shouts and threats pouring down on us from above. Katia looks at the hole, and before I know it, she rips her hands from mine and flings herself out of the ship.

"Katia!"

Boots hit the planks behind me. I climb after her, not even glancing below me before I drop down, down.

The water hits me like a frozen slap.

CHAPTER 7

I gasp and flail my arms with the shock of the cold. My clothes are instantly soaked through and weigh me down, but I have to get to Katia. She's close by, her face white with fear, her sand-coloured braid dark with water.

Faces appear at the hole we blasted in the side of the ship. Snatches of shouted orders carry down to me, but I don't have time to worry about what they're going to do. I kick my legs and head straight for Katia. I can't believe she just jumped like that. She's spitting and gasping for breath, but I get my arm around her and fix the dock in my sights. It seems much farther away now, and the water is choppy. It hadn't looked that way a minute before when I was on the ship.

I keep kicking, pulling Katia with one arm and fighting through the water with the other. I try to twist my head around to see what's happening back at the ship, but it costs too much energy, so I give up. It won't matter what they're doing if Katia and I are at the bottom of the harbour.

Katia tries to mimic me, thrashing her legs, but I dare not let go of her. She jumped in because she knew if she didn't, I wouldn't either. That thought is the only thing that keeps me going. Dirty salt water burns my throat and threatens to choke me, and I can't tell whether we're making any progress. But I keep going.

My breath gets louder than the slap of the waves, and by the time I'm in among the smaller boats docked in the harbour, I'm coughing and spitting water with every breath. My arms and legs are numb. I can't tell if I'm even moving them any more.

Nets and buoys jostle against me, and ahead a small crowd has gathered on the docks. One figure jumps up and down, waving his arms. Feliks. He made it. I head for him, towing Katia, who's floating on her back now, her teeth chattering hard.

Someone drops a rope with a lobster trap attached, and people yell for us to grab on, but I can barely understand what they want. It's Katia who pulls my frozen arms around the cage and forces my hands to cling to the rope. Then we're hoisted upwards in jerky movements, spinning and banging against the harbour wall.

At the top, I fall on to the dock, and Feliks's face appears above mine. He's wearing dry clothes somehow, though I don't have the breath to ask him about it. There's a blur of movement around me, people trying to help. A woman tugs my furs off and replaces them with dry ones that are too big. Feliks thanks her for me—I'm still gasping for breath and coughing.

I turn my head, trying to see Katia through the mesh of legs and baskets. She's shaking hard, her lips tinged blue. I've never seen anything as incredible as what she just did.

"Katia." My voice rasps, full of salt and cold. I have to call three times before people move and she can see me. She nods, trying to tell me she's OK. My vision blurs, and I don't know if it's the stinging seawater or not. "That was the bravest thing ever."

Feliks touches my shoulder and points out to sea.

I haul myself to a sitting position and scan the sea for the ship. It's not hard to spot. Two sailors suspended by ropes hang on either side of the hole we blew in the side of their vessel. Katia can see the same thing, and despite my arms and legs feeling as wobbly as a newborn foal, I smile.

My satisfaction is short-lived. "What time is it?" I ask, looking around at the little group of people surrounding us.

"What a thing to ask!" someone says.

"About half past one," says another bystander—a woman with braids down to her waist.

"Feliks, we need to go. Now," I say.

Katia's already struggling to her feet, water dripping from her braid beneath an old *ushanka* someone put on her.

"Wait!" the woman who put the furs on me calls out, reaching for me as I take off through the crowd.

"Thank you!" I call back in her general direction. We don't have time for anything else—I need to get to the queen.

I keep Katia with me as I run through the narrow streets away from the cold sea, while Feliks lopes ahead of us. We're all slower than usual. My legs burn, and my boots squelch on the packed snow underfoot. I'm clumsy, and my chest feels like it's been broken apart. But there's no way to get this message to the queen other than to take it myself. I have no idea who I can trust any more, which means I can't trust anyone.

We wind through the backstreets and alleys, Feliks pointing the way and steering us right when I'm not sure. Slowly the streets widen and the cobbles clear, and the houses get bigger and give way to shops and businesses. We finally pass the steps of the Great Library and we're close, so close to the centre of the city that I can see the onion domes reaching up past the turret of the ballet school and into an ice-blue sky.

Now that we're nearing the city centre, people turn their heads to stare and frown: three bedraggled young people in ill-fitting furs didn't look out of place on the docks, but we do here.

Finally Katia stops, her hand pressed to her side, and Feliks and I stop too. Her face is white, her hair still soaked dark, but her lips aren't blue any more. I want to urge her on, but the truth is I'm glad she stopped. I bend over, breathing harder than I thought I could.

"Are you all right?" Feliks asks. Katia puts her hand on his back. There's a level of concern on his face I've only seen before when he's asked the same thing of Sasha. I've missed a whole month with them, and now it's clear how close they've become.

I duck my head and can't stop myself wishing I could say the same thing about Sasha and me. I've tried to forget that she didn't tell me about Anatol's banishment, but it keeps slipping into the back of my mind and pestering me like a trapped fly butting against a window.

I take a deep breath, my throat still burning. Once the blood stops rushing in my ears and I can straighten up a little, I notice how busy the streets are. People all seem to be walking in the opposite direction we are. I need to get to the palace, but there are families and groups heading back the way we came.

"What's happening?" I ask a passing girl. I recognise her from the ballet school Sasha and I used to go to. "Halsa, isn't it?"

The girl nods, and I see her gaze flick down and back up again, taking in my wet boots. She's my age, though a whole head shorter. "The queen is visiting the Great Library today with dignitaries from Pyots'k," she says. "There's going to be an address outside on the steps afterwards. Didn't you know?"

I'd forgotten they were here—representatives from the court at Pyots'k, come to pressure the queen about using our ports again. I shake my head.

Halsa frowns. "It's Saint Sergius's Day."

"Yes, of course," I say, as though I hadn't forgotten.

"Back to the library?" says Feliks.

I nod and we all set off, unable to run as the milling crowd gets thicker, but still hurrying. A clot of people stand outside the library. Vendors are doing brisk business from carts. The smell of hot potatoes makes my stomach cramp as I wind through a group of chattering schoolchildren standing in front of an array of musicians. Saints' days are always accompanied by music in the streets and a speech from the queen.

The library steps elevate the building and set it back from the street. All the other buildings look as though they're bowing to it, and well they should—the Great Library towers, cathedral-like, over the rest. Its arched doors rival those at the palace, though its roof comes to a steep peak instead of boasting turrets. Rows and rows of arched windows line every level, and huge golden flagpoles bearing the Demi-dovan flag jut from the façade on either side of the great doorway.

As I reach the front of the crowd, Feliks just behind me, I see the Queen's Guard stationed on the curved stone steps that wrap around the front of the building. They stand at attention in their black furs and gold sashes. The rest of the crowd keeps clear of the steps as if held back by an invisible barrier, but just as Katia appears at my side, squeezing past a woman wheeling a baby carriage, I put my foot on the bottom step.

Immediately two of the Guard move forward. Their crossbows, strapped to their backs, show on either side of their shoulders.

"I must speak with the queen," I say. "It's urgent. She knows who—"

"Move back," says one of the guards, eyeing the three of us.

Both Feliks and Katia do so immediately. Their eyes are cast down, and Feliks turns away.

I step down and pull the oversize borrowed *ushanka* from my head, realizing too late that it doesn't exactly improve my appearance. "Listen, my name is Valor Raisayevna—"

"The queen will address the public shortly," says the guard.

"But I need to speak with her *now*," I say. "It's important."

The guards step back into position, though both keep an eye on me.

"Valor." Feliks tugs on my sleeve. His face is tense, his voice a hissed warning. He's not used to seeing someone speak to the Guard the way I just did.

I let him draw me back into the crowd. The three of us huddle together, our heads close. Feliks is right—Queen Ana told me I'd have to be secretive, and what am I doing? Showing myself in a public place for anyone to see, asking to speak with the queen. I could have got my friends arrested if someone had recognised them.

"Wait until she comes out," says Katia in a low voice. "Then you can signal to her, let her know you have something to tell her."

"I've already been too obvious," I say. "After what you just had to do on that ship. I'm so sorry, Katia." I'm kicking myself for not being more cautious. If Sasha had been here, she would have stopped me.

Katia's eyes are filled with trouble when she turns to me to say something, but then the doors of the Great Library start to open, and a murmur ripples through the crowd as everyone faces them. More guards join the others on the steps. Back inside the library, the queen, the king and the queen's entourage, including the ministers from Pyots'k, are making their way up the mosaic-tiled floor. At Queen Ana's side is a tall girl who holds herself very straight. The *kokoshnik* on her head marks her as royalty. She must be Princess Inessa. A herald announces their imminent arrival on his brass horn, and the street musicians stop playing.

"Valor?"

The voice shocks me—I wasn't expecting to hear it.

"Sasha?" I turn to see my sister, her sharp eyes taking in my clothes and trying to work out how I got this way.

"I'm here with Father. Nicolai's here too, on guard duty. We saw you from the window," she says. "What's going on?"

Of course. My father is in there with the queen.

"Sasha, you're not going to believe what happened to us." I grip her arm, a new plan forming in my head. "Or maybe you are," I add grimly. "I have to see the queen. Or you have to see her, and tell her—"

"Shhh!" A severe-looking woman fixes me with a glare, even as she listens to another woman whose eyes are narrowed at the doors. "How can we trust any of them now?" murmurs the second woman. The first purses her mouth and shakes her head, and Sasha opens her mouth, her eyes flashing, ready to defend our queen. I squeeze her arm, but now the queen and her niece are stepping out through the doors of the library, followed by the king, and the Guard forms a protective semicircle on the lower steps. The crowd hushes, all eyes fixed on the royal party. The swell of people around me pushes me forward again. Numbers have grown since we arrived.

Sasha and I are separated in the press of bodies, me moving involuntarily forward as she goes back. Princess Inessa smiles up at her aunt, and the queen opens her mouth to speak. Just then a crack comes from up above. The crowd gasps as one of the long flagpoles from above the door lurches downwards.

The king calls out, and someone screams as the huge flag drops straight towards the queen. The crowd pulses backwards as I strain to see, but all I catch sight of is the heavy material of the Demidovan flag rippling down from the broken flagpole. Red and gold tapestry billows.

Inessa cries out, and guards rush to help her up. She's cradling one wrist in the opposite hand, her face filled with confusion and fear. My father hurries on to the steps of the library while the king and a lady-in-waiting pull at the flag. People look about themselves while murmurs of "Queen Ana" and "the queen" ripple around. Father's voice sounds, sharp, urgent. "Where is Queen Ana? Find the queen!"

I hear the clock tower in the square strike once, then twice. Two o'clock.

It's plain to see that there's nobody under the flag.

The queen has vanished.

CHAPTER 8

The crowd lets out a collective gasp, and then panic ensues—noble gentlemen clutching their children or their purses, less fortunate members of the population darting away into side streets, knowing that it's the likes of them who might be questioned or blamed.

I'm jostled on all sides but manage to grab hold of Feliks. The guards shout and try to contain the crowd. A couple of them push the Pyots'k dignitaries and the queen's entourage back inside the Great Library. I catch a brief glimpse of my father and the king hurrying with the injured princess between them, and then the doors start to close.

"We have to get out of here," I say to Feliks.

Someone grabs my hand and pulls—Sasha. I see Katia behind her, Nicolai in his Guard uniform visible over her shoulder, and then we're all running. The library doors bang shut, the guards are rounding up people, and everyone is talking or shouting or turning this way or that.

My legs are leaden, stumbling along as though they don't belong to me. I crash into a wide-eyed musician carrying her pear-shaped *gudok* in front of her like a baby and apologise.

"Where are we going?" I yell, but Sasha doesn't hear me over the chaos, so I just focus on dodging the scattering crowd and holding on to my sister's hand. She leads us down a side street next to the library and we run the length of the building, the noise of the guards shouting orders fading behind us.

At the end of the street, Sasha darts left over a low iron railing and straight down some steep steps that I almost miss in the snow. They twist around, so that by the time we reach the bottom, it's dim and we can't be seen from street level. Windblown snow is piled high in the small space, and our boots sink into it. We're all out of breath, but Sasha places a finger to her lips and tilts her head towards a small, obscure door set into the wall.

Our breathing slows, and we all listen. It's quiet on the other side of the door. I nod at Sasha and she nods back, so I twist the iron ring, its cold weight pressing into my mitten. The door opens, spilling snow into the room on the other side.

It's dark, and before my eyes can adjust, Sasha steps in. "This is the special collection," she says, and her voice, even though she keeps it low, echoes. "There won't be anyone down here." We follow her into a cavern of a room filled ceiling to floor with shelves full of leather-bound books and yellowing scrolls and parchments. The air is heavy and thick with the smell of vellum.

Feliks stares around with wide eyes.

I can guess what he's thinking. "These books must be priceless," I say. "How did you know that door would be unlocked? *Why* was it unlocked?" I didn't know this place existed. How many times has Sasha been here and never mentioned it in passing?

Sasha shrugs. "I didn't know for sure. I just hoped it still would be. I have an . . . arrangement with the curator. These books are available for viewing only with prior permission, and— Shouldn't we be talking about something more important?"

I shake my head and shrug off the thought of another part of Sasha's life I know nothing about. It shouldn't matter—it's just the library. "Of course we should," I say.

I lead the other four to a huge oak table in the centre of the room and then try to hide how difficult it is to pull out one of the carved chairs.

"You all saw the flag fall?" I ask. I'm at the head of the table, Sasha and Feliks on my left, Nicolai and Katia on my right. Their faces are grave. They all nod.

"Did anyone see anything after that? Nicolai?"

"I was inside, behind the queen. I'd come to report to her, but I didn't get the chance. There were lots of guards rushing around. So many of them. But I was right there when the flag was lifted up." He shakes his head and slowly shrugs.

"I know. It doesn't make sense. Queen Ana was just . . . gone." I press my hands to my temples. My hair is wet and cold.

Sasha twists her clasped hands, a deep frown furrowing her brow. "Nicolai's right—there did seem to be a lot of guards there. Maybe . . . Perhaps not all of them belonged to the queen."

"What do you mean?" I ask. "You think the queen was *taken*?"

Sasha nods.

I realise she's right—Queen Ana can't actually have disappeared, and she wouldn't leave her duties voluntarily. She's been kidnapped. There's no other explanation.

My sister looks guilty and anxious as she meets my eyes. "We should have stayed, tried to do something."

"Maybe we should have," says Nicolai. "It's our duty to protect the royal family, and we failed."

I give him a hard look. "It was exactly the right thing to do," I tell Sasha. "Who knows what would have happened to Feliks and Katia if the Queen's Guard had questioned them?"

Nicolai opens his mouth and then closes it again, a frown etched on his face. Sasha still looks worried.

"Believe your sister," says Katia. "You did the right thing. With Prince Anatol banished and the queen now gone, who's to say we'll be pardoned? Who's to say we're not escaped convicts?"

Silence drops on us like snowfall dislodged from a roof.

When I look down at my hands, they're clenched into fists. "Anastasia's behind this."

Sasha frowns more deeply. "I wonder if she got Anatol banished just to get him out of the way so she could do this."

"I wouldn't be surprised." My voice comes out sounding weary. I *feel* weary now that we've stopped running.

Feliks shakes his head. "How did she pull this off, though? I mean, it's the *queen*. And in broad daylight." He's half in awe of the sheer audacity of the feat, I can tell.

"Queen Ana can't really have vanished," I say. "She must have gone somewhere. Which means she can be found." I think about the tunnels under the city, about the fountain that I never knew to be anything but a fountain until this week, about the very place we're sitting right now, in a building I've walked past hundreds of times in my life without ever guessing this room existed.

"This library has hidden exits," I say. "I'd bet my life on it."

Sasha's head lifts. "Yes. A lot of old buildings in the city do—not just the palace."

"Do you know any?" I can't keep my voice from sounding tart.

Sasha notices and frowns. "Of course not. I'd tell you if I did."

"So the queen might have been taken through the same door we just used." Feliks rises a little from his seat, though I can't tell if it's from an unconscious desire to bolt for his own safety or to find Queen Ana.

Sasha shakes her head. "I don't think so. There wasn't enough time to do that before we got here."

"There weren't any tracks in the snow, either," I say. "Anastasia must have had some other way."

"And she must have had help," says Nicolai.

"She always does." My sister's voice is sour, and I'm reminded again how Anastasia's betrayal still sits just below the surface with her.

I lean forward, my elbows on the table. "If Father knew of any hidden places in the library, he'd be ordering the Guard to search them right now—"

"He would, but Father mustn't be involved in anything we do here." Sasha's words cut in before mine have finished.

"Why not?" I wait for my sister to speak again, but she just looks at Katia and Feliks for a long moment and then lowers her eyes to the table.

"If you want me and Feliks to leave, we can go," says Katia quickly, but I hear the note of hurt hidden under the hard edge of her voice.

"No," Sasha and I say at once.

"That's not what I meant," says Sasha. "I just meant we can't ask Father to keep all the secrets we're keeping. It's not only the matter of Feliks and Katia's . . . current status. Think about what's going to happen if the queen isn't found quickly. Who's going to stop the Pyots'kan army from marching right through Demidova and using our ports whether we say they can or not?"

"We should just let them," mutters Feliks.

Sasha's eyes widen. "No, Feliks! What do you think they'd do once they gained access to our ports? They'd wage war on Saylas."

Feliks scowls. "I don't care about Saylas. I care about us."

Nicolai blows out a loud breath. "Feliks, if we let Pyots'k use our ports, then the people of Saylas will *know* we let Pyots'k attack them. They'll start fighting with us."

"It would drag Demidova—drag *all of us*—into a war," says Sasha. She looks at Feliks and then pointedly at Nicolai's Guard uniform.

Feliks's face changes, and Sasha gives him a small, sad smile.

"My being in the Guard has nothing to do with this," says Nicolai, his chest puffing up a little. "I don't want a war any more than any of you do, but if I have to fight for Prince Anatol and Queen Ana and Demidova, I will."

"No one is questioning your loyalty, or your bravery," says Sasha.

Katia's head has dropped. I reach out for her and touch her cold hand. "What's the matter, Katia?"

"What will happen to me if Pyots'k goes to war with Demidova?"

"What do you mean?" asks Nicolai.

Katia just shakes her head.

Feliks answers for her. "She's from Pyots'k."

He looks to Sasha. Her face is grave, but she doesn't speak. I don't know the answer to Katia's question either, not fully, but Katia's light skin and hair make it easy to tell she's from Pyots'k. If they cause a war, how will she fare on the streets of Demidova?

"I don't even know anyone in Pyots'k who would want war," says Katia. "It isn't like that. *We're* not like that, but Queen Lidiya . . ." Her shoulders slump.

Everyone is silent for a few long seconds, until Nicolai drags his hands through his hair. "Prince Anatol would never order anything that would hurt you, Katia." He looks dazed, though, as he shakes his head. "And I would never take orders from anyone—"

"You don't know that. You might have no choice. Do you think every member of Queen Lidiya's Guard would want to treat Demidovans badly?" Katia's fingers worry at each other, her hands clasped on the table.

Nicolai sets his jaw, his mouth a stubborn line. "It won't come to it. I studied hard and trained even harder to get my apprenticeship, and I did not put in all that work to become someone who would . . ." He sighs. "I'm sorry, I have to get back before I'm missed. I'll say I was helping round up the crowd. No one will suspect anything with the chaos that's gone on up there. But, Sasha . . . Are you sure I can't let your father know about any of this? If we could get word to someone in charge—"

Sasha shakes her head. "Father will have so much responsibility. Surely you understand, Nicolai, that sometimes the soldiers must protect the general. He needs to be above reproach; he needs plausible deniability."

Feliks looks at me blankly.

I wish I could answer him.

"Plainly put," says Sasha, "I mean our father can't know what we're doing. We'll only put him in danger if we involve him. And if I know my sister, we're going to do *something*."

I start nodding. "The queen didn't ask Father to find Anastasia, she asked me. And she swore me to secrecy— you know that, Nicolai. We can't drag our parents into this. Father needs to keep peace with Magadanskya and with Pyots'k. The less he knows about what we're doing, the better. Then if anything goes wrong, or if we—if we need to do anything he wouldn't think proper—he'll have never known about it."

Nicolai bites his lip, and then nods.

Sasha smacks her hand lightly on the table. "Exactly. And it's like you said, Valor—if Father knows of any possible route out of the library, he'll have ordered it searched, and the queen will have been followed and found by now."

"You should go up with Nicolai and find out," I say. "Father will give you access. He'll tell you what's happening."

"True. And it's been too long already; he'll worry if he can't find me."

Sasha pushes her chair back, the sound echoing loudly over our hushed voices in the chamber. She and Nicolai hurry away, and for long minutes Katia, Feliks and I sit. I begin to feel the ache in my legs, the bruises on my elbows, the cuts and scrapes on my hands, and the deep, deep tiredness that weighs down my whole body.

Sasha finally comes back, quiet and alone, her pace giving away the fact that she doesn't bring good news. The queen hasn't been found. Father doesn't know how she was taken, or where, or why, but he's in the archive hall now, issuing a constant stream of orders while every alley, spire and cobblestone of the city is searched.

"So are there really no other ways out of this building?" asks Katia.

Sasha shakes her head. "No, there *must* be a way, Father agrees. He just can't find it. There are things only the members of the royal family know, but the king has no knowledge that can help. In fact, Father could get very little out of him—it's such a dreadful shock after Anastasia, and then Anatol being accused." She presses her lips together, pity and worry mixed on her face. "Father told me to find you, Valor, and go straight home. He would have had a guard take us if any could be spared." Her shoulders slump as she takes a seat at the table again, but mine tense as I realise what has to happen.

"Anatol," I say.

Feliks frowns.

"There are some things only the members of the royal family know. If Anastasia knew of a way out, then she must have learned it from the queen, and if she learned it from the queen—"

"Then perhaps the prince knows too," finishes Sasha. Her eyes are bright again.

My mind is whirring, picking up speed. "Who do we ask about having him released?" I look to my sister.

"I don't know." She wraps her arms around herself. "I don't know what's going to happen without a queen on the throne. But by the end of the day, Father will."

"We should be at home waiting when he gets back," I say. "If we're going to keep my mission to find Anastasia a secret, he and Mother can't know about what happened today. They'll never let us out of their sight again." I gesture towards my damp and ill-fitting clothes.

"You're right. We should meet up again tomorrow, but we should go now. You can tell me how this happened on the way." Sasha shakes her head as though she can't even begin to fathom how the three of us ended up this way. I don't blame her.

Hearing Sasha mention Anastasia—how raw she still sounded—makes me regret asking her whether she knew anything more about passageways in the library. I touch my sister's arm as we head for the door. "It's fortunate you knew about this place."

"Fortune bred of spending much of the past thirteen years here," she says. It's only a slight rib about the fact that I've spent precisely none of the past thirteen years here, but it's enough to harden my feelings again after how things have recently been between us.

"Maybe your father and the Guard will find the queen quickly," says Feliks. "Then we won't have to do anything at all."

"Maybe," I say. But for some reason I don't believe it.

I don't think any of us do.

Sasha nudges me awake. When I move, everything hurts, and it takes me a few seconds to remember that I'm at home, still sitting upright on my bed. At least I'm wearing clean, dry clothes—I vaguely remember tugging them on after we sneaked into the house right before Mother got back. She still questioned me closely about where I'd been. Sasha had to answer, because I had no idea that I'd spent the day safe at target practice, honing my rusty crossbow skills after the trip to Magadanskya.

"Father's back," says Sasha. Her face is guarded, tense.

I scramble off the bed. We've been waiting hours for our father to return—at least I judge it to be hours by how dark it is outside.

Sasha runs along the landing to the top of the stairs. Our parents' voices are coming from the kitchen downstairs. Something in their tone makes us both falter. We look at each other and stop, an unspoken agreement stilling us and making us sink down near the top of the stairs instead.

I rest my head on the railing. Sasha, two steps above me, leans forward, her elbows on her knees.

". . . delicate situation . . . unease . . ." Father is pacing, and his voice drops in and out of range.

Mother's voice is easier to hear. ". . . terrible . . . disaster for the country. What are we going to do? They must find her. There'll be chaos without a queen, and no heir in Demidova—"

She stops abruptly. I look back at Sasha. She frowns and shakes her head.

"What is it?" asks Mother.

"There is an heir."

Father's voice is clear now, as if he's stopped pacing. I can picture the deep crease between his eyebrows.

"Inessa Alistratova, the queen's sister's second daughter. She's not next in line, but we can't wait for the elder daughter; we must restore order as quickly as possible. It's our only chance to continue to stave off Queen Lidiya of Pyots'k and maintain our links with Magadanskya. If either sees our position weakening . . ."

I turn to Sasha. The crease between her eyebrows—a softer version of Father's—is as deep as I've ever seen it.

"Any regent would be walking into a difficult position. There's already so much work for her to do," says Mother. "Isn't she injured?"

"Yes, although not badly. She's young, though, and timid, from what I've seen. She'll need a lot of counsel." Father just sounds tired now, as if the thought has reminded him of all that's happened today and all he still has to do.

There's movement in the kitchen—footsteps on the stone floor. Sasha and I rise and pad quickly back to our rooms. We no longer need to ask Father who has the power to release Prince Anatol.

On her first day in office, we'll have one more matter to put to the new queen regent.

CHAPTER 9

My breath huffs out fast as Sasha and I weave through the crowded streets near the palace in the early morning chill. Everybody's out. Everybody's talking. Nobody's paying attention to a group of street performers with painted faces. The festival for Saint Sergius's Day is supposed to last all week, but it's been overshadowed and all but forgotten now.

Both Mother and Father were up and gone before Sasha and I rose. They left a note with strict instructions to stay in the house this morning until they return. Neither of us likes deceiving them, but Sasha says it is for the greater good.

That's true, but I don't think she would have said that a year ago.

My whole body aches. I have a new and unrivalled appreciation for dry clothing—and an old yet still surprising appreciation for my sister's powers of persuasion. We left the house this morning in complete agreement that we needed to gain an audience at the palace today, but now we're almost at the gates and we still don't agree on what we should say when we get there.

Sasha looks over at me. "We *have* to tell her about the mission Queen Ana entrusted you with, Valor. She's queen regent—ruler of the whole country. And she's not going to lift the banishment on Anatol and let us do whatever we want just because we say she should. She barely knows us at all."

I keep my voice low. "We've been through this already. I don't see why we have to blindly tell the queen regent everything. I don't see why we even have to decide what to tell her right now. Can't we see what she says when we get there?" Maybe it's my time in Tyur'ma that makes me feel uneasy, makes me want to hold things back until I'm sure I can trust someone.

"Nobody enters a conversation like this without having thought it through first," says Sasha.

"Sometimes you just have to react in the moment," I mutter, though I know she'll never change her mind.

As we clear the last street and enter the central square, I catch sight of the golden gates of the palace and the onion domes rising above them. The snow has been cleared, and our boots hit cobbles as we make our way to a back entrance that Sasha knows.

We pass through it unchallenged—Sasha's been here before, and a few words to a guard who recognises her gain us entry—though for some reason my heart beats fast, like I'm some kind of criminal. I can't quite shake that feeling, though I never truly was one.

We scurry down a long, narrow passageway, then up a flight of stone steps. I hear a high voice falter and then speak up again, and then we're out in the palace proper, among a group of Father's colleagues in the great hall with its mosaicked floor. The room is full of advisers in the blue cloaks they wear—I'm not sure I've ever seen so many gathered together all at once.

Father himself must be here somewhere, though I can't see him. And I definitely don't want him to see us. Sasha and I hang back by a marble pillar, our heads lowered. But no one's paying any attention to us. They're all listening to the girl at the front of the room.

She wears a dark, sombre dress and stands on a platform flanked by two guards wearing purple sashes. I don't see much of the small, chubby girl I vaguely remember in her. She's as tall as I am and trying to stand like the queen does, though her wrist is bound in a silk sling tied around her neck.

I think we've entered at the finale of her speech, because the first thing I hear her say is, "Rest assured, I am here to do everything in my power not only to stand in as queen regent and make sure our fine country is safe but also to ensure that the rightful queen is restored to the throne as swiftly as possible." She almost rushes through the words, as though she's memorised them and is glad to finish.

Then she bows her head, the diamonds on the *kokoshnik* she wears glinting in the many lamps that burn along the length of the hall. The assembled advisers bow back. I tug Sasha behind the pillar.

We wait until the room clears, watching as advisers, some clutching papers, break into clumps and hurry away, talking to one another. I don't see Father, but as I sneak a look around the pillar, I do see the queen regent heading back into a separate chamber. The door shuts with an echo, and we're alone in the great hall.

"Now's our chance," I say.

We steal across the room, glancing left and right, and knock at the door.

"Enter."

Sasha wipes her palm on her trousers and turns the knob. The queen regent sits at a desk, upright in her brocade gown. She's maybe a little older than we are, tall but slightly built. She looks like someone who's trying not to look anxious, and I don't blame her one bit. As Anastasia's cousin—and not even firstborn—she must never have expected to find herself thrust on to the throne.

"Queen Inessa." My sister bows low, and I remember myself and do the same.

The queen regent looks at us expectantly. Her dark eyes are set deep and ringed with thick black lashes. "And to whom do I owe the pleasure of this visit?" she asks.

"We met briefly yesterday," says my sister. "I am Sasha Raisayevna—"

The queen regent rises immediately. "Yes, of course! And this must be Valor! I have met your father and heard much about both of you already," Inessa says warmly. "He helped me with that speech, although I'm afraid I didn't do it justice."

I can't help but smile before I recall why we're here. "We've come on a matter of great importance," I say.

Inessa tilts her head, equally concerned and interested as I explain about Anatol's banishment and how we believe he could have vital information about the route used to spirit Queen Ana away, and therefore also about where she might be now.

When I'm finished, Inessa, who has been nodding encouragement throughout, takes my hand in her uninjured one. "I am so pleased that you came to me, and that my dear cousin has such loyal and protective subjects. You can be sure I will act on this immediately. But . . ." She lowers her voice, leaning forward. "What do you think I should do?"

Sasha clears her throat delicately. "Perhaps bringing Anatol back to the palace would be a good idea."

"A very good idea," I say, much louder than I meant to.

Sasha gives me a quick look, but Inessa just nods, seeming relieved and grateful. I'm glad to know she's going to do something, but I can't help feeling a little stab of disappointment that it will be she who releases Anatol, and the two of them together who unravel what happened to the queen.

We all stand there awkwardly for a few seconds.

"Thank you for seeing us," says Sasha. "We'll leave you to make arrangements."

"Oh, yes, of course!" says Inessa. She inclines her head, remembering her royal bearing, and Sasha and I again bow low.

"Would you like us to—?" I was going to ask her about my orders from Queen Ana, if I should continue the search for Anastasia, but I suppose the task of finding the queen and finding her daughter are one and the same now. "Never mind," I say.

I follow my sister back out into the great hall, but when we're halfway across, a small murmur makes both of us glance over our shoulders at the same time.

Inessa's head is bent towards an attendant, her hand delicately shielding her mouth. The attendant's eyes are trained on us. I glimpse the scene for only a second before another attendant glides forward and swiftly closes the doors.

I suppose that's it. It's in more powerful hands than ours now. "Come on," I say. "We're late to meet the others."

We're both quiet as we hurry back the way we came, threading our way through the square and out into the side streets to a snow-filled alley. Nicolai waits for us, his dark eyes watchful under the black *ushanka* of his uniform. He nods, and though we stay a short distance behind, we follow him to a narrow passage between two houses.

Katia's already there, stamping her feet, her pale hair tucked out of view under her *ushanka*. Feliks jumps down from a fire escape above when he sees us.

Nicolai glances up at the clock tower, just visible over the roofs of the houses. "I don't have much time. I'm on duty soon at the house where they're keeping Anatol."

There's no one around, but I still look both ways before I speak. "We've been to see the queen regent."

All eyes shoot to me.

Katia lowers her head, raising her eyebrows at the same time. "And?"

"And . . . she said she'll deal with everything."

There's a pause, and then Feliks grins. "That's great. Even better than we expected."

Sasha elbows him. "You're very eager to trust in the monarchy all of a sudden."

That raises a smile from Feliks, but Katia's forehead wrinkles and her mouth purses. "Are you sure that we can trust her?"

"Yes," I say firmly. "She even asked us what we thought she should do."

Sasha nods. "She listened to us."

Katia lets out a sudden breath. "Our pardons might come through," she says. And for the first time since I've been back in Demidova, I see hope on her face.

Sasha takes her hand. "Of course you'll get them now. Just as soon as Anatol helps Queen Inessa to find Queen Ana, he'll be back in his position working to overhaul Tyur'ma, I'm sure of it."

Katia's hope disappears as though it's been washed from her face with a bucket of cold water.

I can't stand to see it, not after what she did on that ship, not after everything she's been through. "We'll get them now," I say.

Sasha and Feliks stare at me.

"Right now," I say. "Inessa's going to release Anatol. Nicolai's heading there. We'll go with him, and when Anatol comes out, we'll be the first to speak to him, before he even goes back to the palace."

Feliks knocks Katia with his arm. "Yes!" And Katia smiles, a full-on, eye-crinkling smile that has the rest of us joining her.

Nicolai looks to the clock again and then awkwardly at Katia. "I'll have to leave you before we get to the gates. If any other guards see me, I won't be able to help Anatol."

"We're *all* helping Anatol," I say, still rubbed the wrong way from my conversation with Sasha.

Nicolai opens his mouth, but Feliks jabs him in the ribs. "Can't be seen consorting with known criminals. Don't worry—we get that all the time. Come on, let's go."

Nicolai smiles, half grateful, half embarrassed.

On the way, Sasha and I tell Feliks and Katia about what we overheard from our parents. Katia wants to know all about Inessa, so Sasha fills her in, right down to the slippers on Inessa's feet and the inflections in her voice. The whole time we're walking, I'm happy just to watch Katia. She still keeps her hair tucked away, but she seems lighter. When the house comes into sight, my nerves tingle. But Nicolai was right—we can't let the rest of the Guard see him with us, or let them see Katia or Feliks until Anatol comes out. I can't risk some overzealous officer questioning what we're doing here.

We leave Nicolai on the road and move behind a snow-bank up on a hill to the right of the house. There's already movement at the rear, in the garden, and I pull Sasha down next to me, behind the fallen trunk of a tree. Snow is piled deep here, and the four of us crouch low. Feliks begins digging out a little trench, and Katia helps him. But my eyes are locked on to the scene below. As I watch, four guards arrive through the gate at the back of the garden, joining the two who already stand near the walls of the house. There are three more at the front of the house, where Nicolai has disappeared. They all wear deep purple sashes, not the gold of Queen Ana's Guard. They belong to Queen Regent Inessa.

"We won't have to wait long," I tell Katia. "Queen Inessa has sent her guards already."

A frown flickers over Sasha's face, her eyes flitting from one guard to the next.

"What?" I ask her.

She doesn't answer for a few moments. "A lot of guards, don't you think?" She casts a questioning glance at me, and I count them. Now there are eleven.

"There's no carriage," says Katia. "Are they expecting him to walk?" Her voice says she doesn't think that can be right.

"Maybe the new queen just wants to make sure her cousin is very, very safe," whispers Feliks.

I nod. "That makes sense. And I'm sure there's a carriage on the way." I look back down the street, but I don't see any horses yet.

I don't see any horses twenty minutes later either, when everyone has gone quiet. There's a sinking feeling in my stomach.

"Do you think Nicolai's all right?" asks Feliks.

"I don't know," I say. "I don't know *what's* going on. But maybe Anatol does."

Katia shakes her head. "What good does whatever he knows do us if he's still stuck in there? He's not coming out. Why isn't he coming out?" Her shoulders slump. Her arms creep around her knees the way they did back on the ship. Feliks crouches next to her, but his eyes are on me.

I won't let her be that afraid again. I won't let her down, not ever again.

"I don't know," I say. "But the four of us broke out of Tyur'ma when no one had escaped from there in three hundred years." My heart beats fast and hard. "This is one boy from one house. How hard can it be?"

CHAPTER 10

An hour later, we're all stiff and cold and still crouching behind the log. I have a stomach full of churning needles. The Guard has rotated once, but at no point have there been any less than eight of them outside the house. I haven't taken my eyes off the grounds, and I know there's no way in.

For the first time, I let my gaze wander upwards. What am I going to tell Katia and the others? They've alternately watched the house with me, sighed, fidgeted and looked to see if I'm going to move or speak or do *something*.

I press forward, snow compacting as it flattens between my furs and the tree trunk. I've been focusing on the grounds, but the house has walls. And windows.

And a roof.

I explain to the others what I mean to do.

"It's awfully high," says Katia.

"I could get up there, easy," says Feliks.

"But you're not going to," I cut in quickly. "I am. Anatol doesn't know you."

"But I'm sure all the Peacekeepers in Tyur'ma remember you just fine," adds Sasha.

Feliks bites the inside of his cheek. "OK, you go, then. But once he's out, you'll need somewhere to hide him, and that's with us. The thieves' network can keep him out of sight better than anyone else in the city." He tips his head towards the heavily guarded house. "And it looks like he's going to need it."

I can't believe it's come to this—can't quite believe that Queen Ana is gone and her traitorous daughter has escaped. I don't know why Inessa isn't doing what she said she would. When I got myself arrested and sent to Tyur'ma, all I could think of was my sister. Now Demidova itself needs my help. The weight of it presses down on me until I think I might panic.

But I nod at Feliks, and we split up—Sasha and Feliks to the woods behind the house, Katia to the street at the front.

"Will you be all right?" I ask her.

When Katia nods, I see the same determination on her face that I saw when we ran through the tunnels under the prison after our escape. Even when she's short with me, even when I wonder if she's been through too much and is going to give up, she keeps going. It makes me rein in my own doubts and keep them inside. It makes me want to be as stubborn as she is.

I wait alone behind the log, keeping my breathing even, forcing myself to focus. It's quiet for minutes that feel more like days, and then the sharp crack of a branch in the woods carries on the crisp air.

I watch from my hiding place. The guards haven't moved, but I don't need them to. All I need is for their attention to stay where it is now—trained on the line of trees that borders the garden.

I vault the log and run full tilt down the hill towards the side of the house. I scramble over the fence, drop to the other side, roll and land back on my feet, barely pausing before I run again. I don't have time for stealth, just speed. The side of the house looms closer. It's a flat slab of stone, the only windows high up on the second floor. My boots sink into fresh snow, but I still slam into the wall harder than I wanted to, my palms slapping the stone. I press my cheek against its solidity for one second, and then glance both ways before I rip off my mittens to grasp the drainage pipes that run from the roof down to the ground.

A steady trickle of water gurgles inside the pipes, melting snow from last night's fall. I pull myself up fast, out of breath already, my pulse pounding in my neck. My boots scrabble against the stone, and I haul myself up, gaining brief footholds on the brackets that hold the pipe in place and relying on my hands the rest of the time.

My arms start to shake. I glance up—only halfway. At any second I expect to hear shouts or the whistle of arrows, but soon all I can worry about is my numb fingers, how they don't feel like parts of my body any more, and how I'm relying on them to hold me up here. I'll break like dead wood if I fall.

Another crack sounds from the woods, and I jerk my head towards it. My fingers loosen and I slip precious yards down the pipe, clamping my jaw shut so I don't cry out. I'm not going to last much longer.

I stop being careful and just pull as hard as I can, hand over hand, ignoring the stinging pain in my fingers and the burning in my arms and legs. My breaths come short and fast, and then I'm up, level with the gutter, pulling on it, not caring if it creaks or groans as I use the last of my strength to haul myself on to the roof.

I lie flat on my back, my eyes closed. Everything hurts. But I have to get up and get this done. I force myself upright, my arms weak and trembling, and pull my mittens back on. The roof is flat, edged in stone and covered in a thick coating of snow. The wind whips across it, flinging strands of hair across my face. How am I going to find a way in? I can't shovel the snow across the whole expanse of the roof with my bare hands. I take a cautious step forward and my boot sinks down until it hits stone.

Hurriedly, I walk forward in a straight line, taking even steps. Each time my foot meets stone, I continue tracking back and forth, stepping as though the roof is a chessboard and I want to land on every square. Eventually I trip on something raised, something that sounds different when I catch myself and stamp on it.

I drop to my knees and scoop the snow away, brushing around the edges until I've uncovered a maintenance hatch. I get down on my stomach and pryise it open a little way. It's dark inside, and stale, but warmer air hits my face. There's no sound or light, so I heave the hatch fully open and peer down.

It's an attic. Empty.

I sit on the edge of the hatch, feel my stomach clench at the thought of the drop and ease my weight out into the void. I land with a muffled thump, and a bolt of pain shoots up from my ankle.

The air is musty, tickling at my nose as I wait for the pain to fade. Then I steal over to a set of folding ladders on the floor. There's another hatch beneath them. I hold my breath and ease it open. The light from the hall below is glaring, but there's no one around.

I quickly slide out the ladder and sneak down it. Voices come from the bottom of a spiral staircase farther along the landing. I push the ladder back up before I lose my nerve. The click as it slides into place has me gritting my teeth, but I spin around and make for the first door I lay eyes on.

I make it into the room and swing the door closed, catching it just before it slams. Then I still my breathing, the very tips of my fingers holding the door open a sliver, as the voices come closer. I have to fight the urge to run. Just swallowing makes so much noise that I'm certain they'll find me.

They walk past, two of them, both wearing Inessa's purple sashes. The grounds are overrun with her guards, and the house seems to be too. Where's Nicolai?

Every muscle in my body is tensed. But at least I know where I have to go to get to Anatol. I take a deep breath, then another, and peek around the door to make sure the coast is clear.

I slip out of the room, feeling instantly exposed. The thick carpet muffles the sound of my boots, and although my heart beats right out of my chest, I fly down the staircase to the ground floor, then keep going, swift as a hare, to the door under the stairs and down again to the cage where we found Anatol before.

It's dimly lit and damp, but unguarded. I steal along, out of breath, until I see him. "Anatol?" I breathe the word, barely a whisper, but he whips around as if I've hit him with a crossbow bolt. The shock on his face has to be mirrored on mine—he's dirty and dishevelled, his hair an unruly mess, and his blue cloak is stained and grimy. He doesn't look like Prince Anatol at all.

"Valor?" He rushes over to the bars of the cage, his eyes darting to the wall behind me.

Keys hang there, out of his reach.

But not out of mine.

I slip them off the hook and unlock the cage. His eyes go wide, and he steps through the open door.

"Have you seen Nicolai?" I whisper.

He shakes his head. A surge of anger at Anatol's plight pulses through me. I put my finger to my lips and then point upwards. Anatol gives a short, sharp nod, and we're off, back through the door under the stairs, back up towards the attic. We're halfway there, a chandelier burning bright overhead, when I hear a woman's voice. Someone laughs.

I stare back at Anatol behind me. He looks even worse in the light, deep shadows under his eyes and a dark cut on his bottom lip. His face is frozen with a fear that jolts me back to Tyur'ma and Warden Kirov.

What have they done to him?

And what will they do if we're caught now?

There's nowhere for us to go, so we wait, half crouched. My hands are clenched into fists. At the top of the stairs, two guards walk past. My heart beats so loudly that I don't understand how they can't hear it, but then they're gone, and we run up the stairs.

I pull on the cord that releases the sliding steps up to the attic. Anatol is almost beside himself now, clutching his hands together and throwing fearful glances up and down the hallway. But the ladder swings down smoothly, and we're up and pulling it back into place in seconds.

I let out a big breath and we wait, staring at each other, expecting shouts, waiting for the ladder to be wrenched down again and for us to be discovered.

Nothing happens.

We're going to get away with it.

In the dim light from the open hatch to the roof above us, I smile. Then a quick flash of horror passes through me and I look up. I jump up and reach as high as I can, but I already know it's pointless. I can't reach the hatch. It's way above our heads, and the attic is empty. No barrels like on the ship. No cannons. No anything.

Anatol follows my gaze and tilts his head, as though he can't believe I leapt down here with no thought as to how I'd get back up.

"We can still get you out," I say. "Climb on to my shoulders."

It's risky—if we fall, the noise will alert the guards. And even if we don't, I doubt we'll actually reach the hatch, though I don't tell Prince Anatol that.

But he shakes his head. "It's way too high, and I'm not leaving you here."

"And I'm not leaving *you* here," I say. "What kind of rescue would that be?"

He raises an eyebrow.

I frown. "Well, it would be an even worse one than it is already."

That makes him smile a little, though he winces and touches his lip.

"Valor, I'm more than happy to see you. I can't think of anyone else who'd even try to do this for me. Did you say Nicolai was here? Did he help you get in?"

I shake my head, the worry that must be on my face making Anatol frown.

"I think he's in the house somewhere. At least, I hope he is. The only way he'll stay safe is if everyone here still believes he's just an apprentice in Queen Ana's Guard. He can't help us."

Anatol presses his lips together and peers into every dark corner, though it's plain to see there's nothing here. I don't join him. I'm still sorting through a dozen variations on a plan to get out of here.

But the truth is none of them will work.

There *is* no way out.

CHAPTER 11

Prince Anatol shivers. We sit side by side on the boarded floor of the attic, and his movement reminds me that I'm cold myself. The light from the hatch is starting to fade. It's only a matter of time before someone goes to check and finds Anatol gone.

Something hits my shoulder, and I flinch and clap a hand over my mouth. Anatol jerks away from it. I listen for sounds from below even as I look for what hit me.

A knotted rope dangles in the gloom, and above it, Feliks's face peers down from the hatch. He waves his hand wildly, and I find myself waving back, energy and hope pouring back into me.

"Well, go on then," I whisper to Anatol.

He grabs the rope and gives it a tug. It holds, so he starts climbing. I keep it taut from the bottom and watch as he disappears over the edge of the hatch and on to the roof, and then I follow. My arms are still weak from my earlier climb, but I don't care. I just want to get out of here. In no time, I emerge into the crisp air, and Feliks pulls me on to the roof, the snow there still crisscrossed with my tracks.

I flip the hatch shut and look up to find Sasha, Katia, and Feliks all standing there while Anatol sits in the snow, staring at each of them in turn. Without a word, Katia starts piling snow on top of the hatch and packing it down hard. It's a good idea, so I join in.

"Thank you. All of you," I say. "I don't know what we would have done if you hadn't come."

Feliks shrugs. "It's what we do. No one gets left behind."

"I can't thank you enough," says Anatol. "I've been frantic. My guards all changed today, and I heard them talking about what happened to my mother. When they first came downstairs, I thought I was to be released." He touches his lip. "But that's not what they did at all."

Feliks shakes his head. "Prince Anatol, do you think you can climb down? It took a while to get up here, and it'll take even longer to get down with two extra people." He looks to me.

I feel like I've just stepped off the roof and am waiting to hit the ground. I could almost laugh. But with so much resting on my thinking clearly, I can't afford to lose focus, even for a second.

"Have you seen Nicolai?" I ask.

Sasha packs an armful of snow on to the pile over the hatch. "He was turned away while we waited for you," she says. "He and two other members of Queen Ana's Guard. They were the last of the gold sashes to leave, and Nicolai didn't look happy about it. He had no choice but to walk away, though." She stands up, surveying the packed snow.

"He did the right thing. The last thing we need is any suspicion falling on him. Let's go," I say.

Feliks leads the way back over the edge of the roof and down the way I came. He makes it look easy, though I know it's anything but. No alarm has been raised, no guards have run to or from the house. That's good for us—better luck than we've had since Queen Ana charged me with finding her daughter—but it means no one's gone to check on Ana-tol yet. And someone has to check on him eventually.

I watch as Katia follows Feliks, pressing her lips together so hard that they lose all colour. When I ask Anatol if he's OK, he just nods and takes his turn.

"Go on," I say to Sasha.

She shakes her head. "Not this time, Valor. You go now. I'll follow you."

We're both thinking about the desperate, exhausted run we made under the city by the docks when we escaped Tyur'ma. Sasha refused to leave me and make her own escape. I insisted she go first then. Now I don't argue; I just look down to the ground in time to see Anatol joining the others back on the snowdrift behind the fallen log. Everything's hushed and muted, and no sound comes from the guards. A wolf howls out beyond the city limits, faint and far away.

I drop over the side and descend, far faster than I climbed up. When I reach the bottom, I make for the fence, stepping high through the snow, and heave myself up. My stomach growls and my mouth is dry. I land hard on the other side and steady myself, crouching against the cold iron railings.

Sasha is halfway down the wall when her foot slips and she falls, silently. It's me who makes a high-pitched sound, which I cut off as I leap to my feet. Sasha hits the ground on her back, crumpling into the snow, landing so hard that she almost disappears in the indentation.

I grasp the bars, ready to scale the fence again, calling her name as loud as I dare. She doesn't move. A picture of Sasha lying in the snow in Tyur'ma after Feliks pulled her out of the ice dome forces itself into my head, bringing with it the same terror I felt then. I fumble the climb, unwilling to take my eyes off her, unable to think about what I'm doing in my worry.

A guard appears from the back of the house, and everything goes into slow motion. I whirl around and yell, "Run!" at the other three hiding behind the log, then spin back and scream, "Sasha!"

She moves, struggles up, but my relief barely has time to register before the guard shouts and starts running towards her.

"Get up!" I scream. "Run! Run!"

I cling to the fence now, unable to do anything as Sasha starts to run, painfully slowly.

"Come on, come on," I plead, willing her towards me. The guard is gaining, and another has appeared behind the first.

Sasha's breaths fog the air fast, but her steps are slowing, her face twisted in pain.

Three voices start shouting with mine from behind, calling her name, telling her she can do it. Sasha's head lifts up, and she staggers the last three steps to the fence, and then I'm pulling her as hard as I can, dragging her over.

She cries out as we both land on the other side, but there's no time to stop. I look left to the woods and then right to the street, but Feliks is yelling to follow him, so I sling Sasha's arm around my neck and we take off to the right.

Over my shoulder, I see the front door of the house open and guards run in and out. If they didn't know Anatol was gone before, they do now. I face forward and keep going. Sasha leans most of her weight on me, which throws off my balance, but I keep going and going and going, until at last Feliks stops.

It's only then that I notice we're in the alley where Feliks and Katia met us that first day we came back from Magadanskya.

No one speaks for a full minute. I crouch in the snow, my back to a wall, the sky darkening above us.

"Are you OK?" I ask Sasha.

She hasn't got the breath to answer yet, so she just squeezes my arm.

Anatol holds his sides, breathing hard. "Tell me, then. Tell me everything."

I tell him about Inessa—how we told her Anatol could help find Queen Ana. His face darkens, and he looks more like the Prince Anatol I met in Tyur'ma—the one who scared me with his determination.

Everyone's eyes are on Anatol.

"What is it?" I ask. I'm fervently glad at this moment that he's on my side.

"Inessa's always liked to get her own way without actually having to do any work herself. But I'm surprised she had the nerve to lie to you," Anatol says. "She's always been peevish about being fourth in line, but she never dared speak about it in front of Anastasia. She always just fawned and giggled and twisted her hands in that nervous way.

"But I know she never had any intention of releasing me today. Her guards have loose tongues. I couldn't make full sense of what they were saying before, but now I can. She intends to do precisely nothing to get Queen Ana back."

Katia and Feliks look to me, and my cheeks heat. Inessa lied. And she made me believe her.

Sasha's hands clench. "But she's making public proclamations that she's doing everything in her power." She's still out of breath, and her voice is laced with pain. I stand by her side and let her lean on me.

Prince Anatol shakes his head, his face grim. "I have no idea what's going on, but she doesn't want my mother found."

Inessa's not going to help us. She's going to try to stop us. But I made a promise to Queen Ana. I look up at Anatol. "Your mother was at the Great Library when she was taken. We know there are secret passages that are known only to the royal family. Do you know where they are? Do you know how Anastasia or . . . whoever she put up to this could have made Queen Ana vanish like that?"

Anatol frowns. "I don't—no, wait." His frown deepens and he stares at the snow, focused on memories the rest of us can't see. Finally, Feliks fidgets, and Anatol shakes his head. "I think I might. But it was years ago when I saw it. And Mother wasn't showing me, she was showing Anastasia. I wish I'd paid more attention, but so many of the things I learned were really intended for the future queen. I was just there out of convenience. And in the library, I always gave the books more attention than anything else. What does my father say?"

We all look to Sasha. She bites her lip. "Your father didn't know. My father says he's been very upset since the queen . . ."

Anatol's face softens into worry. "He handled Anastasia's betrayal differently from Mother. He's barely spoken about it at all." His voice drops low. "Or about anything else."

I glance up at the sky. The sun has dipped, barely visible above the buildings. I touch Anatol's arm. "We have to take you to the library."

Katia nods her agreement. "If you see it, you'll remember."

"But *none* of us can afford to be seen in public now," says Anatol.

Feliks nods to my sister. "Sasha knows a way in."

"OK, then let's go," says Anatol. He takes a step forward, and his knee almost buckles.

Katia puts her arm around him, practically holding him up. "You're in no state to go anywhere right now. None of us are."

"We'll hide him here," says Feliks.

"Valor, we *must* get home," says Sasha. "Mother and Father will be frantic. If they've told anyone we're missing, and if anyone suspects Anatol's escape had anything to do with us, we could end up back in Tyur'ma. Our parents could face worse than banishment this time."

She's right. We can't risk the library now. We must get back. "We'll do it tomorrow," I say to Anatol. "First thing. I promise."

Sasha and I don't talk on the way home; only dogged determination keeps us going, heads down, boots moving mechanically, until we get there. She's limping, and I have to keep stopping to put her arm around my shoulder and help her along.

When we reach the back door of the house and slip inside, we pause and look at each other. We hear voices from the front of the house, the exchange of greetings and pleasantries.

One of the visitors says something, and then Father's clear voice carries back to us. "I believe they're in their rooms. As you know, it's not been long since we returned from a rather lengthy journey to Magadanskya . . ."

Sasha and I don't stop to hear the rest. Quickly, we ditch our furs, shoving them into the cupboard. I wrench off my boots and throw them in too, then smooth my braids.

"Your boots!" I hiss at my sister as the voices head towards us.

Sasha bites her lip and shakes her head. There's no time to run to our rooms, so we hurry to the kitchen instead, Sasha dropping into a seat at the table while I yank glasses from a cupboard and pretend I'm in the middle of making us drinks.

"Valor?" My mother's voice sounds slightly on edge.

"In here," I call, trying to calm my own voice.

"We have the honour of a visit from Queen Inessa," says Mother.

I lose my grip on the glass in my hand and only just catch it. Water splashes on to my fingers. Sasha's chair scrapes over the stone floor.

"Please, no need to rise," says Inessa, holding out one slim hand.

"Your Highness," I say, dipping into a bow.

"Valor." She inclines her head.

"Please take a seat," says Father, stepping to the table to pull out a chair.

"Don't trouble yourselves. I have only come, as I said, to make sure that the girls are quite safe." She smiles in the nervous way she did back at the palace, twisting her hands together and then holding them at her sides as though she's been caught by a deportment teacher who's rapped her on the knuckles for behaviour unbecoming of a princess. "I came as soon as I heard Prince Anatol had escaped his banishment. I blame myself, of course. I should have left the palace immediately after Valor and Sasha told me he might have information about where Queen Ana has been taken. Now I'm afraid it seems evident that the accusation of him being in league with Anastasia was correct, and my aunt was quite right to banish him."

Father's eyebrows go up when he hears that Sasha and I went to see Inessa, but before he can say anything, Inessa turns to him, her eyes huge and sorrowful. "*Both* of my cousins at fault, and my aunt missing. I can't imagine what Uncle Fillip is going through. But I'm so glad to find that Valor and Sasha are here, as you said, and safe."

"Thank you for your concern, Your Highness," Father says. "We're so honoured that you would travel here yourself when one of your attendants could have done the job for you."

The queen regent smiles. "I couldn't possibly have handed this task to anyone else. I will try to measure up to my aunt's example, if only in this small way, and serve Demidova on the front line."

Sasha, who has been as still as a hunter, shifts her weight, pressing her lips together.

"You're quite sure you've been here all day and haven't seen anything unusual?" Inessa says, looking at my sister. "I would be more than happy to send some of my personal Guard if you feel in danger in any way. Who knows what the prince may have on his mind—whether he knows you came to see me earlier."

I can feel the barbs in her words, like little fishing hooks.

"I've neither seen nor heard anything of import," says my sister evenly. "We've been upstairs reading for the larger part of the day."

Inessa's gaze drops to my feet and stays there. I glance down. The hems of my trousers are wet.

The queen regent turns to Mother and smiles. "Thank you so much for welcoming me into your home."

I don't hear the rest as she turns and my parents accompany her to the door with all the attendant polite words. At the front of the house, Inessa's guards wait to escort her to her carriage.

I stand stock-still. Sasha's face is tight. We look at each other, but neither of us speaks. We're waiting for Mother and Father to come back. When they do, I notice that Father's still wearing his blue cloak—he must have returned from the palace very recently. Mother, however, is wearing clean trousers. I can't smell horse or dog, which means she hasn't been out on the plains today. She might have been in the house at some point—might know that Sasha and I have been gone since early this morning.

Father strides to the table and starts gathering up the papers I hadn't even noticed were there.

"Are you . . . returning to the palace?" asks Sasha. I can tell by her cautious tone that she had expected a second questioning at least.

Father frowns. "Your mother and I both are. Prince Anatol is missing. Queen Ana is missing. The king is all but—" He shakes his head, cutting himself off. "The queen regent has requested our presence. The country is in crisis." He mutters the last part to himself, thrusting the gathered bundle into his leather bag and hurrying away. I'm glad he's too distracted to question why we went to see Inessa without speaking to him first.

Mother is fastening her thick riding cloak.

My relief mixes with guilt. We lied to our parents, and to the monarch of the realm. I don't dare ask Sasha if that's treason, or something even worse. We watch silently as Mother pulls on her leather gloves, drops a hurried kiss on to each of our heads and follows Father.

In the doorway, she stops. "There is to be a guard posted here tonight," she says. "So don't think for a moment that you'll be going anywhere else today—*or* that we won't be discussing where you've been since this morning when I return. I've been out looking for you for the past two hours. Whatever you're doing, stop it now, before you get in any more trouble than you already are. I wish I could stay with you, but the guard will be here. Just a precaution." Then she smiles a tight smile that reassures no one of anything and is gone.

"A precaution against what?" I turn to Sasha, but her shoulders have slumped, and she holds her head in her clasped hands.

"Sasha?"

"It's my ankle." Her voice is full of every second of strife we've been through today.

I run around to her side of the table and lift her boot into my lap. She keeps her hands pressed over her face as I unlace it, but when I try to ease it off, she grips the sides of the seat.

"I'm sorry," I say as I tug gently. She nods, her face tight. She knows I feel it as much as she does. When I finally get the boot free, she lets out a whimper.

Her ankle swells right in front of my eyes, a huge bruise blooming like a purple rose from the bone outward.

"Oh, Sasha. Why didn't you say something?" But I know she couldn't have. There was no time. All the way back home, and throughout the entire conversation with Inessa, she had to bear the pain.

"What are we going to do?" I ask.

Sasha shakes her head. "This is the least of our worries. Inessa knows."

It feels like the last fire inch-stick tossed on to a pile I can't hope to keep balanced. "Let her know as much as she likes," I say with a bravado I don't feel.

"I would," says Sasha, "but what did she do when she realised we were lying to her?"

"She ordered our parents to her side," I say. I swallow. Inessa could have called us out on our lies, could have accused us, but she chose to do something else entirely. I feel sick.

I open my mouth, but I can't think of anything comforting to say. Father thinks the peace Queen Ana strove for so

long to bring to Demidova is at risk. We're no closer to finding Anastasia or Queen Ana. Instead of showing the new
queen that Anatol is a trusted ally, we turned him into a
wanted criminal, along with Feliks and Katia. My sister,
who I swore to always protect, is tensed in pain, and there's
a guard outside our house.

CHAPTER 12

I wake up suddenly, the light to my left confusing me for a second before I realise I'm not in my bunk at Tyur'ma. It's just dawn breaking outside my bedroom window. I didn't hear Mother or Father come back last night, but in truth, I might not have heard anything had our house been set upon by ravenous wolves or an entire army of Peacekeepers.

I slip out of bed and go to the window. A guard with a purple sash stands in the garden below. I can't see her face—only the top of her *ushanka* and the braids snaking out beneath. She looks up, and I retreat and hurry straight to Sasha's room.

She's lying with her ankle propped up on a cushion, and though her eyes are closed, she opens them the second I step into the room. She grimaces as she sits up.

"The guard is still here," I tell her. "Did Mother and Father come back?"

Sasha rubs one hand over her face. "No. Inessa is keeping them busy at the palace, no doubt. She's trying to show us we can do nothing while she goes right ahead and takes Queen Ana's place."

Sasha sounds unusually bitter, so I try to lighten her mood. "As if we don't have enough trouble with Princess Anastasia trying to do the very same thing." I realise my mistake as soon as I say the words. There's no joking about this.

I sit carefully on the bed so as not to jostle Sasha's ankle. It's swollen, and the bruise has spread like a dark stain.

"Sasha, I know what Mother said, and I don't want to worry her, but . . . we can't just leave the others out there."

"I know, but I can't do anything today, even if we could get out of the house," she says, dejection all over her face.

I plump her cushion for her, and it comes to me in a flash, an idea darting like a winter hare in the snow. "No, *you* can't leave the house. But you can still be all the use in the world."

I explain what I mean, then run off to my room to get ready. When I'm done, I stash my boots and furs by the back door and then run back to Sasha's room.

"Ready?"

She is, so I help her up, and we make our way slowly along the landing and down the stairs. Sasha hisses and leans her weight on me, making my aching muscles protest. At the bottom of the stairs, I lower her to the floor.

She gives me a nod, and I run up to the top of the stairs and fling a pair of Mother's heavy leather riding boots down to the bottom. I rush after them as they thump on the steps, and Sasha lets out an ear-rending wail.

"Help!" I shout, shoving the boots under the stairs. I run to the back door and swing it wide, but the guard is already there, her sword half drawn.

"It's my sister," I pant. "She's fallen."

The guard sheathes her sword, metal sliding on metal, and hurries after me into the house. I lead her to where Sasha lies on the floor, clasping her leg.

The guard bends and frowns as she examines Sasha's ankle. "When did this happen?"

My heart kicks up. She's not going to believe us.

"Yesterday," says Sasha at once. "I thought I could bear weight on it today, but I was wrong."

The guard nods, her frown clearing. Sasha widens her eyes at me.

"I'll fetch a doctor," I say. "Unless you think it would be OK to leave your post? I'm sure we'd be quite safe if you did."

The guard narrows her eyes at me. "I'm not leaving my post. You go."

I take soft steps backwards towards the door, then turn tail and run. As I snatch up my furs, I hear Sasha say loudly, "Oh, be careful. It hurts."

There's a recurve bow in the cupboard, along with a set of Mother's gloves, and once I've pulled on my furs, I grab both. This bow's not my favourite. It's a good-enough weapon, but it's not from my own set. My crossbows and bolts were a gift from my mother when I started my apprenticeship, and I lost both of them—the first when I got arrested and sent to Tyur'ma, and the second when we were captured and put on the ship. It hurts my heart—they were such beauties, and I don't know how I'm going to explain my only remaining set's absence if Mother notices.

As I ease the door shut, I glance around quickly and then run full-tilt away from the house, stopping in at the doctor's house to send her to Sasha, then taking the most direct route into the city and back to Feliks, Katia and Anatol. Inessa will no doubt find out what I've done, but I have to do it.

I pause when I reach the marketplace, stepping to the side of the busy thoroughfare to let shoppers pass. A maid from a grand house running errands hurries past carrying a basket, and she pauses too. Inessa's guards are stationed around the market and the square beyond, their unfamiliar purple sashes standing out. There are no musicians, no performers, no people out just to see the spectacle of the festival in the city. There *is* no festival. The maid and I lock eyes for a second, and I see the wary look on her face before she presses her lips together and moves away.

I pull my hood low and keep my head down as I pass two guards. The swords at their sides are shorter than those Queen Ana's Guard wears. They seem less . . . ceremonial, somehow. I wind through the cobbled pathways, wondering if the traders' calls are more muted, if the people really are casting furtive glances at the guards, or if it's just my jumping nerves.

I settle a little once the streets grow quieter. I'm almost at the alley when someone grabs my arm and pulls me into a narrow space between two buildings. I wrench away, swinging my hand over my shoulder to grab my bow.

"Stop! Not again," the stranger whispers furiously. He flings back the hood of his cloak.

I drop my hand to my side. "Nicolai? I was coming to find the others. We didn't know what had happened to you. I—are you in disguise?" He's not wearing his Guard uniform, clad instead in an entirely different set of clothes than he had on yesterday—old, coarsely made, dull in colour.

"There are guards *everywhere*," he says. "And not the ones I work with. Queen Ana's Guard has been told to stay in the barracks and wait for orders, and apprentices have all been sent home. Anatol sent a message to me, though, telling me where he was. You didn't come back to him, so we were trying to get to the Great Library, but when the square filled up with guards, I told Feliks and Katia to keep Anatol out of sight. I've been trying to find a way to get to you."

"You haven't got very far," I say.

Nicolai looks taken aback.

"Sorry, I mean, where are Katia and Feliks, then? And Anatol?"

He blows into his cupped hands. His mittens are thin, and his face is flushed darker by the cold. "At the library already. Feliks wanted to sneak in and find out for Sasha how Queen Ana could possibly vanish the way she did. And," he adds hurriedly, "for you and Prince Anatol, and the whole realm, of course. Katia said he wasn't going alone, and Anatol refused to take orders from either of them and stay put, so . . . here I am, trying to get to you."

He bites his lip. "You're right, though—I wasn't doing a very good job. I'm used to *being* one of the Guard, not hiding from them." He looks anxious, unsure of himself. "I always thought it was black and white whose side I was on. Now there are two queens . . ." He shakes his head.

I touch his arm. "Come on," I say. "We have to get to the library, and that's all there is to it. Follow me. I'll take you there."

He pulls his hood into place and we slip on to the streets, keeping our heads down and blending into the crowd of shoppers and workers and palace servants moving through the city. I keep Nicolai behind me whenever I see Inessa's guards' distinctive tunics anywhere near us.

When we reach the library, we skirt around the guards standing watch outside and head to the back entrance that Sasha showed us.

I heave my weight against the door, but it doesn't give. Nicolai joins in. But this door is locked now. "We'll find another way," I say with confidence I don't feel.

We sneak along the rear of the building, keeping tight to the great blocks of stone, peering in every window, pulling back when we see librarians or one of the few scholars who have received special permission to be here since the queen disappeared.

"There!" In the sixth window, I catch sight of furs and a pale braid, barely visible behind a tall stack of books teetering between two thick shelves. "Katia."

At least, I hope it's her as I tap on the window, quietly at first, then growing more insistent until it jars the bones in my hand.

Feliks pops his head around the books, and his eyes go wide. He hurries over to the window and pulls it open, Katia helping him tug on the huge frame. I give Nicolai a leg up and then scramble after him, dropping snow and a couple of arrows from my quiver on to the floor in the process.

Katia puts a finger to her lips, and I snatch up the arrows and kick the snow away. The four of us hurry silently back to the fortress of books where Feliks, Katia and Anatol are hiding.

"Have you found anything?" I ask them.

Anatol shakes his head. His lip is bruised around the dark cut, and he looks just as tired as yesterday. In fact, they all look tired.

"I think it has to be somewhere on the ground floor," says Feliks.

"And I say it could be anywhere, but we have no idea unless Anatol can tell us. After all, he knows best," says Katia. Her legs are folded awkwardly under her like a foal's, and she flicks one braid over her shoulder.

I look between the three of them. Anatol and Katia don't look back at me. I frown at Feliks. He rubs a hand up and down the back of his head as if he's angry with his hair. "Prince Anatol sent a message to Nicolai last night."

"I know," I say. "Nicolai told me. And?"

"And he *had* to send a message," says Feliks. "Never mind whether it risked the network or not. Couldn't do without his manservant for one night. Mila was *furious* when she found out."

Nicolai stiffens at my side. "I am not a manservant. I'm a Queen's Guard," he says hotly.

"Are you?" asks Katia, looking his threadbare clothes up and down. "Because it doesn't look like it to me."

"I had no intention of risking the network. That's not what I meant to do at all." Anatol sits stiffly on the floor, but his tone tells me he's said this repeatedly, probably since last night.

Feliks opens his mouth again but I hold out my hand, wishing fervently that my sister was here. I have no idea how to sort out what's going on, but I do know we can't do this here and now.

"We really need to hurry," I say. "And Katia's right—we can't find what we're looking for if Anatol can't help us." I nod at him and try to summon up a reassuring smile that doesn't start Feliks off again.

Anatol looks around, frowning. "I've been here so many times that . . . well, I don't think there's any part of the library that I *haven't* been to," he says.

"Think harder," I say. "You might have been everywhere, but it would have to have been a time when Anastasia and Queen Ana were here too."

"Where's Sasha?" asks Feliks. "She's the best person for this."

I explain why she's at home and watch concern crease Feliks's expression. Anatol remains deep in thought.

The prince's hand shoots up. "Genealogy!"

Feliks's mouth hangs open a little, and I suppress a sudden, inappropriate laugh. He looks like a quizzical puppy.

"It's where they keep all the records of my family. Royal births, marriages, deaths, coronations. It's right at the top of the library. We had to spend hours there learning our family history, and then Mother took Anastasia off for a few minutes while my tutor had me copy out a list of every allegiance and advantageous marriage every prince of Demidova has made since saints know when. I remember wondering at the time what Mother and Anastasia were doing."

"That sounds promising," Katia says. Her eyes are hard, though, when she looks at Anatol.

I nod. "Let's go."

I lead the way and peek out of the door. The library is full of large open spaces and tiny rooms, staircases with wooden banisters and recesses filled with great tomes and small pocket books. I always favoured the map room whenever I was dragged here by my sister—at least the maps are useful—but I still know my way around the place pretty well from all the times I'd had enough and searched through it in growing frustration to find Sasha.

Anatol pulls his hood up and we put Nicolai behind him. Then I swing the door wide and stride out into a corridor and up a little-used flight of wooden stairs as though we all belong here. We pass a scholar clutching dusty scrolls who turns to look after us, but I keep my head high and hope she doesn't check with a librarian to see whether we're supposed to be here.

Up and up we go, but I don't slow until we reach the closed, carved doors of the genealogy room. I hesitate. This area isn't open to the public except by special consent.

"Let's not hang around," hisses Feliks.

Anatol steps around me. "Here. It's my family; I should be able to go in there whenever I want, even if I am an outlaw now." He pulls on the polished knobs, and the doors glide open. We all slip inside, and a draught wafts into my face as the prince swiftly closes the doors behind us.

In front of us stretches a huge room, its walls covered with thick drapes and gilt-framed portraits. Carved wood and marble lecterns hold huge gold-leaf-edged books in rows all along either side of the room, and in the centre is an aisle of glass cases filled with jewels and *kokoshniks* and sceptres that rival and even surpass Queen Ana's.

Feliks's eyes are as round as two gold coins.

Anatol nips out of an alcove containing a bronze bust on a marble pillar and into one displaying brightly bejewelled eggs. "Come on!" he says, breaking the spell. His voice echoes off the high arch of the ceiling. Katia and I exchange a glance and a nod. She goes left, and I go right. We lift drapes and peer behind bookcases. Feliks drops to the floor and looks under the thick rugs, while Anatol paces the room, frowning and occasionally reaching out to touch a globe or staring at one of the books that lie open to a page of his family history. Nicolai sticks close to the prince, his hand occasionally moving to touch the hilt of a sword that's no longer there. I glance at him now and then—he looks certain and steadfast with his duty laid out plainly in front of him.

After an hour, we've covered every inch of the room, crossing one another's paths and checking everything someone else has previously looked at.

"I've already opened that," I call to Katia as she pulls at the front of a great glass clock. All the brass workings are on show, bright cogs and levers at work behind a sparkling etched-glass case. It would be big enough for a person to stand inside if the clock's innards were removed. I opened it only with the same dwindling hope that Katia's obviously feeling too.

"It's not here," says Feliks. "Anatol, are you sure this is the right place?"

We all wander into the middle of the room. Anatol shakes his head. There are two bright spots of colour on his cheeks—just like those his sister has when she gets angry. Except I don't think he's angry. I think he's embarrassed.

I know what it's like to feel out of place, like I did in Tyur'ma, like I did at the Magadanskyan palace too, after being a prisoner. Anatol's never been anywhere but the palace. Being taken to that house and being rescued only to find that he had to hide with the thieves' network can't be easy for him.

"What use is he if he can't remember anything?" demands Feliks.

"Can't get us pardons either," mutters Katia in a sullen voice I haven't heard since our time in Tyur'ma.

Nicolai draws himself up to his full height. "Don't speak to Prince Anatol that way."

"Stop it!" I try to think of the best way to put it so Feliks will understand, but how can I tell him what one night with the thieves might have been like for Anatol when he and Katia have spent a month with them just to try to help us all? When this is Feliks's *life*?

Anatol almost stamps his foot, but stops himself. "I can't remember anything else!"

"We're doing something wrong, then." I use my calmest tone, the way Sasha would, and try to think the way Sasha would, but my mind doesn't bend into the same shapes hers does. I look around the room. There's nothing we haven't examined or moved, prodded or pulled. Where can it be hidden?

"This is pointless. It's too hard," says Feliks.

I freeze. "No—it's not hard *enough*."

Feliks looks at me blankly.

"Maybe it's not hidden at all. Maybe the answer's right in front of us."

I look around the room again. The book atop one lectern is closed. Every other book is open. I run over to the closed book, and the others follow.

I open the book, and something clicks. All five of us twist our heads towards the sound. The others' faces are expectant, bright with hope.

I run back across the room. "Here!" The glass clock case stands a fraction ajar, and when I wedge my fingers into the gap, the whole thing swings open. Behind it a steep stone staircase spirals away into the dark.

Anatol and Nicolai crowd in behind me. There are odd grooves in the stone on either side of the entrance, as though there should be a banister slotted into place, but it's missing.

I take a deep breath and step into the narrow space. Anatol follows, and we spin down and down, leaving the light behind. Just before it disappears, I find a scrap of material snagged on the stone wall. I pull it away and wordlessly hand it over my shoulder to Anatol. I can't see the colour, but it feels like fine silk. Fit for a queen.

Anatol's footsteps stop for a second, and then he hurries after me.

After a while, there's a grating sound from above, like a blade being sharpened on a whetstone but heavier. I keep going, but unease spreads across my chest, making my skin prickle.

"Valor?" Katia's voice sounds uncertain but loud in the tiny space.

"I don't know," I say. "Just keep going."

"Something's coming," says Feliks. "I can feel it."

He's right. There's a draught, and the grating is louder; now it sounds like stone rolling over stone.

"I think . . . I think maybe—" Nicolai's voice rises in panic.

"What?" I quicken my pace without waiting for his answer. Our feet fly down the steps, fast breaths drowned out by the sound behind us.

Katia lets out a yelp, but I can see light ahead and fling myself forward, missing the bottom step entirely and sprawling on to a damp stone floor. Someone grabs me around the waist and flings me to the side just as Feliks and Katia fly down and dodge to the side of the staircase.

On their heels, a huge stone boulder comes rumbling and rolling out, its momentum carrying it straight ahead beyond us.

I stare after it, breathing hard. "Is everyone OK?"

We all scramble to our feet.

"What in all the saints' names was that?" asks Feliks. "And where are we?"

I look to Anatol, but he doesn't know. A stone-walled tunnel stretches in front of us, the dark punctuated by the occasional lit torch affixed to the wall.

I take a torch and adjust my bow on my back, and we press on. Before we've taken five steps, the wall to my left seems to move. I jerk my hand back.

Anatol, instantly alert, appears at my side. "What?"

"I don't know." I hold the torch close to the wall. The bricks move, sliding back and forth as though someone's pushing them one at a time from the other side.

I look at the torch in my hand. "Maybe I shouldn't have picked this up."

The wall begins to ripple, stone grinding on stone.

"Run!" Anatol pushes me forward and I run, the flame on the torch flaring backwards and sending shadows flickering around us. The tunnel grows narrower, and the shifting bricks snag my sleeves until I'm almost pinned as I fight my way forward.

I burst out into a dark space at the same time a cry comes from behind. Anatol barrels into my back, and we both fall on to the floor. I twist around to see the bricks meshed across the opening of the tunnel, as if someone built a wall and poked out every other brick.

Feliks, Nicolai and Katia are on the other side.

A noise behind us makes me whip back around. A figure moves across the cavern. I push up on to my knees.

"Anastasia!"

CHAPTER 13

I call out Anastasia's name before I've ordered the thoughts in my head. Anatol is already on his feet. I dropped my torch when I fell, and it hisses a thin trail of smoke into the air, but the cavern is lit by other torches. Anatol's face is drawn. He takes a step forward, and I pull him back. His foot is right at the edge of a steep drop into black water that quietly laps against the stone.

His sister's form throws a huge shadow on to the back wall of the cavern, but she stands as still as a statue of a saint, her hands held neatly in front of her. I stare around the cavern, greedy for a glimpse of the queen, excitement rising after the shock of coming face-to-face with the princess.

This is my chance to make everything right. I can capture Anastasia and rescue the queen. When I do that, everything else in Demidova will fall into place.

"Valor," Anastasia says, her mouth twisting as though my name is out-of-date pickled cabbage. "And, of course, my brother. I shall forget what it is to see either of you apart from the other."

Anatol's chest quickly rises and falls. If the body of water weren't keeping him from her, I think he'd have arrested her himself by now.

I'd be delighted to join him.

"Where's the queen?" My voice echoes in the large cavern, and I spot a boat bobbing on the water farther down. Whether it's a slow-moving underground river or a man-made canal, I can't tell, but it's far too wide to jump, and I can't see any way across. There must be one, though. If Anastasia got over, then I can too. My heart thumps at the thought of it.

Anastasia lets out a cold little laugh. "The queen is somewhere *you'd* never think to look." She takes a few steps forward to the stone banks of the water. I keep my shoulders square and angle myself to face her as she moves so she can't see the bow at my back. I'll use it if I have to, but I'd rather keep the element of surprise for now.

"Oh, Valor. You didn't think she was *here*, did you?" The amusement and scorn make me wish I could reach out and shake the princess. But this is what she wants—to make me angry, to distract me, the way she did in the palace when I caught her with the stolen music box.

I won't let her do it this time.

I force the annoyance away. I have to keep a clear head and let her talk while I figure out how to get to her. I nudge Anatol, who startles so hard that I wonder what he's been thinking this whole time. He looks at me, and I widen my eyes.

"We knew Mother wasn't here," he says, turning back to his sister. "In fact, you left such an obvious trail leading to this place that we thought it might even be a false one altogether. Evidently we gave you too much credit."

Anastasia's cold smile barely slips, but it's deeply satisfying to hear him needle her anyway. I almost can't tear my eyes away, but I need to find a way to her. I'm faster, I'm stronger, and I'm going to make her take us to Queen Ana.

"Really?" says Anastasia, adopting an air of mock interest. "It certainly took an awfully long time for you to arrive here, given that it was so easy." Spiteful glee lifts her smile as she looks over to Katia, Feliks and Nicolai. "Did something happen on the way to slow you down?"

I don't move, but while Anastasia's eyes are on our friends, I squint into the darkness and look for a bridge. When I don't find one, I scrutinise the walls and the ceiling for ropes or pulleys, anything that will get me to her. I could swim, but it would be too slow and obvious. I need speed. My hands itch to grab her.

"Nothing of any real import," says Anatol carelessly. I don't know how he does it after everything his sister and her greed have put us all through.

I spot some steps leading down the inside wall of the bank, the kind that would ordinarily lead to a mooring. But these seem to drop straight into the water. It doesn't make sense. I stare at them hard, wondering if . . .

I inch forward—the same steps are cut into this side of the bank too.

"Anyway, we could ask you the same thing," says Anatol. "It hardly seems as though you're doing well, hiding in a dank cave. A far cry from the throne room."

Anastasia just smiles again. "Needs must, brother. I'll have what I want soon enough."

"What *do* you even want any more?" I ask. She can't have the throne—Inessa has it.

Anastasia looks at me as though I've said something ridiculous. "I want what's mine by right of birth. And I'll have it, too."

"You won't," I say. "You can't." Doesn't she know Inessa is queen regent? I decide to hold the information back, just in case. Maybe I can use it somehow.

She leans forward a little, staring right at me. "It's not as though anyone's been able to figure out my plans or stop me so far. Even the palace dungeon couldn't hold me."

"That's true," I say. "There must be some who are still loyal to you in the palace."

A wicked smile flashes over her face. "And wouldn't you like to know who it was who helped me escape."

"Tell us who." Anatol's voice is deeper and rougher than I've ever heard it, and he doesn't wait for an answer before he speaks again. "Where's Mother? Where have you taken her?"

I wish he sounded like the Prince Anatol who questioned me in the tower at Tyur'ma, haughty and commanding. He doesn't, though. He sounds angry and desperate and hopeless and all the things I felt when Sasha was taken away from me and before I made my plan to be arrested and sent to Tyur'ma.

"Well, you're *so* clever, Anatol. Just as clever as Sasha is—isn't that what Mother used to say to the two of you? Surely you can work out where Mother is, or at the very least who helped me escape. Come now, think very hard."

The smug tone of her voice pushes all the restraint right out of me.

"I couldn't care less who it was, and neither does he," I say, jabbing my finger at Anatol. "All you've succeeded in doing so far is putting your cousin Inessa on the throne, and if you think she's going to hand it over to you, then you're as deluded as you are selfish."

I feel better for at least three seconds, but then Anastasia laughs. "They'll be celebrating my coronation the day I take the throne. You really don't understand anything, do you, Valor? Honestly, it makes me wish your sister were here. At least she'd appreciate my plans, even if she didn't have the guts to do anything about them. Where is Mother's little pet, anyway? Don't tell me you two aren't nested together like *matryoshka* dolls any more. What *will* Mother think if Sasha isn't simpering over someone? She won't recognise her."

The last of my control evaporates. I rush to the steps and down them, ripping my bow from my back as I run. I step out, an arrow nocked, with no thought for whether I'm right about the way across the water.

My boot sinks up to the ankle, then hits stone. There's a bridge all the way across, linking the steps, but it's concealed underwater. The current hits me harder than I expected—this must be a river after all—but I lock my muscles rigid, point my bow at Anastasia and keep stomping right across the bridge.

"Am I to be your prisoner?" asks the princess. She still sounds calm, but I know she can't be, not with two of us and only one of her, and me with my bow. "Where do you intend to take me?" She arches an eyebrow at me.

I don't slow as I reach the steps on her side, but in my head I'm casting about for an answer. I can't take her to the palace; Inessa might have Anastasia locked away with a triple guard, but she'd never make her tell where Queen Ana is, not when she wants the throne for herself.

"Maybe I'll hand you over to a friend of mine named Mila," I say. "I'm sure her associates would be very pleased to see you." Let the thieves' network keep her locked up. She'd have no allies among them. They might have no love for her mother, but they'd have even less for her.

"Valor!" Nicolai's warning bounces off the walls of the cavern.

A hand clamps over mine and forces my bow down. I try to spin around, but someone else grabs me from the other side. The tip of my arrow scrapes the stone floor, and I find I can't release it now, not that it would do any good.

On either side of me, Anastasia's guards hold me rigidly in place, wresting my bow from me. It clatters to the floor, and one of them kicks it into the water. They're dressed all in black, with no sashes. On the other side of the river, Anatol's eyes flash defiance over the wide hand that covers his mouth. Two more guards flank him, pinning his arms to his sides.

"Let him go!" I struggle and then drop my body weight to the ground, but the guard won't let me fall.

Princess Anastasia hasn't moved a step, but now she claps her hands together. "Well, as much as I have enjoyed this reunion, I really do have less tiresome people to talk to."

She turns, then pauses, her braids flicking back over her shoulder. "You didn't actually think I was alone down here, did you?"

I renew my efforts, twisting my wrists, trying to kick the man and woman who hold me. They don't even look at me.

Anastasia walks to the boat at the back of the cavern and hops lightly into it. "By the way, Valor, I was here only to retrieve something I left behind. You had perfect timing in that respect. A great pity you couldn't get here any earlier." She holds up something that glitters in the light. Anatol makes a muffled sound. It's a *kokoshnik*—Queen Ana's. The one she was wearing the day she was taken from the Great Library.

I scan the boat again. There's a tiny window in the cabin, and inside, something—some*body*—moves.

My heart stops. The queen was here the whole time.

I throw myself at my captors, first left, then right. Anatol thrashes around too, but neither of us can get free. Anastasia casts off. The boat moves instantly away on the black water.

And all I can do is watch it go.

CHAPTER 14

My eyes are watering from strain by the time I lose sight of the boat, but the guards still hold both the prince and me. Eventually I stop fighting and stare at the ground. Everything I've been chasing since I got out of Tyur'ma was right here in front of me for the taking, and I lost it.

I'm held in place for long minutes, miserable and sullen, feeling the tender patches on my skin throb. So much struggling, and all I'll have to show for it is a collection of bruises. How am I going to tell Sasha that I was this close and still failed?

Eventually, the two guards let me go. I look up, surprised. "Don't follow us. We have orders," one says, letting the light glint on her sword. Without another word, they walk away along the riverside tunnel and unmoor a small rowing boat that must have been nestled behind Anastasia's vessel.

The other two guards who were holding Anatol follow, and the four of them push off. Even if I could follow them, Anastasia's long gone by now.

I turn to face Anatol, wondering what I can possibly say. He's sitting on the ground like a broken doll. Feliks and Katia's dejected faces show through the chinks in the brick wall, and Nicolai looks ready to break through his cage with his bare hands if he could. Feliks's fingers grip one of the stones, and his eyes, settled on Anatol, are round and sorrowful. It's like a sharp pinch to the heart.

I rub my wrists and arms, shivering as water drips from somewhere high above. I should search the cavern while I'm on this side of the river. I should galvanise myself and the others, tell them this is only a setback, that we can still find the queen and stop Anastasia.

The other four look at me. I stand up straighter even though I don't feel like it, and then march over to where I first saw Anastasia.

"You can't follow them!" Katia calls.

"I know. But we have to search the place." I say it with false conviction, then lift one of the torches from its bracket and walk briskly up and down the cavern, following the far wall. It's uneven, with plenty of alcoves where the guards could have melted into the darkness when we arrived.

I pause. Anastasia could have hidden too, but she didn't. She wanted to toy with us. With me. I kick myself again for being one step behind her all the way. Then I stumble into a barred iron door, and it clangs backwards into the rock. A hand reaches out to steady it. Anatol. His boots drip on to the ground.

He stares into the cell in front of us and swallows. It's so like the one I lived in at Tyur'ma that I'm glad Katia isn't here to see it. It sends a shiver down my back and leaves a look of mingled horror and sadness on Anatol's face. Had his mother been in here since she went missing?

"She's not in there any more," I say, but the words are limp and just make me wish Sasha were here to say something better.

"I should have done something more about Anastasia." His voice echoes softly, hollow and empty. "I knew she resented the way Mother and I would talk. But I . . ."

His gaze drops to the ground, and he swallows.

I touch his arm. "You what?"

"I liked it," he says. "Sometimes I thought Mother was paying attention to me to make sure I didn't feel left out and useless. We all knew I would never have a real role in life and that Anastasia would be queen. But Mother *liked* me. She wanted to talk to me." He raises his eyes to meet mine. "And I liked it. I liked the attention. I liked— Valor, I liked it when Anastasia was jealous."

I squeeze his arm. "But you didn't know it would drive her to this. How could you? Your mother loves you. She's *supposed* to love you, whether you're going to lead the country or not. Anastasia's jealous of anyone who comes close to your mother. This isn't your fault, Anatol. It's hers."

He looks at me, heartbroken and serious. "I have to stop her. The country needs its queen back. And *I* need my mother back. I know I can never rule, but I can make up for—"

"Stop talking like that," I say. "There's nothing for you to make up for, and we *are* going to stop your sister and get your mother back. Come on." I tug Anatol's arm until he backs away from the cell. "There's nothing here."

He stops and stares in the direction his sister went. "Where do you think she's gone?"

I think about it. Where do all rivers lead? "To the sea."

He nods. "You're right. It can only lead straight out to the coast."

"You want to go after her?"

His shoulders slump. "If this heads to the sea, it heads to open water. We have no boat, and Anastasia could have sailed in any direction."

That's exactly how I feel—completely at sea, with no idea which direction to go, despite my words to Anatol. I march back to the bridge and barely feel the cold water as it flows around my ankles again.

Anatol follows, and we both go back to the wall where the others are trapped. Feliks has pushed his face against the stone so hard there's an imprint on his chin. It must have been just as difficult for them to helplessly watch the princess escape all over again as it was for Anatol and me.

"I'm sorry," I say. "I should have known I couldn't outwit her."

Katia's head lifts. "But how could you have even known she was here?"

"Katia's right." Anatol puts his hand on my shoulder. "None of us knew Anastasia had guards with her. None of us suspected the queen was here. It's not your fault they got away." He forces a small smile at his repetition of my words to him.

It feels like my fault, though—especially when I look at Anatol's face. How sad he is, how much older than his thirteen years he seems.

"You miss your mother," says Feliks, his voice so quiet I almost don't hear it.

Anatol nods, and all at once he's a young boy again, a boy whose sister has betrayed him, who has no home to return to and whose mother is gone. Feliks's thin hands wrap around the bricks on either side of his face, and I'm reminded of when I first got to know him in the palace dungeon.

"I know how you feel," he says, still in that same small voice.

"Where's your mother?" asks Anatol.

I remember Feliks showing me the scar he got in the forge, remember him telling me that he worked there after his parents died, and my heart gets so full that I have to look at the ground.

"She died when I was young," says Feliks. "But I remember her. She used to sing to me when I couldn't sleep."

I think of my own mother, of her strong hands pulling a bowstring, sharpening a knife, brushing my hair.

Anatol stands up straighter, the prince in him showing through again. "I'm sorry," he says. "I'm sorry she died. It's not so bad for me. I know my mother's alive."

I stand up straighter too. "And you have friends who will help you find her," I say. I hold my torch close to the bricks. "Look for a way out of this," I tell Katia, and then I do the same on my side, scouring the wall for something that will show me how the mechanism of the bricks works.

Anatol joins me, and together we run our fingers over the wall until I find a stone that's a little shorter than the rest and push it in. Immediately the bricks start to fold back the way they came. Katia steps forward.

"No!" I say, hastily pulling Anatol out of the cavern and into the space where the others have been stuck. "We all stick together, and we all go back the same way."

Nicolai nods. Katia takes my hand. Feliks and Anatol look at each other for a moment, then down and away.

"What now?" says Feliks as we start back the way we came. I've never seen him knocked down for long, not since the first day I met him.

"Now we find out who let Anastasia out of the palace dungeon and we question them," I say. It's the only thing I can think of, though I don't let myself dwell for too long on how little it is.

"I can help with that," says Anatol, and he sounds much brighter. "I know all the palace staff, and I think most of them even like me."

"Won't they have been questioned already?" asks Katia.

Anatol nods. "They have been. But that was right after it happened. Someone must know something, and that's a big secret to keep for this long. After what's happened this past month, maybe there's someone at the palace who just wants to spill their secrets to someone they can trust."

"But you can't go to the palace," Feliks says. "It isn't safe for any of us any more."

Anatol sets his jaw, a determined prince. "I won't need to go to the palace at all. I know exactly where we can start."

It's late by the time I get home. The house is dark and silent, but even though I'm tired and my boots are still wet, I duck behind a pine tree and look for the guard. I strain my eyes into the darkness for minutes on end. Nothing moves.

I slip around the house, flitting from one hiding place to the next, but it soon becomes clear that there is no guard. No one is posted at the house any more. I was expecting more guards, not fewer, after the way I got out this morning. I dread to think what Mother and Father are going to say. I'll have to tell them everything. My skin prickles as I open the back door.

"Valor?"

I jump at my name and suck in a big breath. Sasha sits by the kitchen fire, though it's burned low. Her injured ankle is neatly strapped now and rests on a cushioned footstool.

"What did the doctor say?" I ask.

"It's only bruised," she says. "Badly, and it will hurt for quite a while, but there's no worse damage."

I let out a breath. "There's no one outside. Where's the guard?"

Sasha looks as drawn and tired as I feel. "When you didn't return along with the doctor, our guard sent out a message. When she got an answer, she just left without telling me why. But putting a guard here didn't work—you got out anyway. So . . . Inessa's found another way."

She holds out a folded letter.

My stomach clenches.

I pull off my boots and drop them quickly in front of the fire. I can barely see, so I throw more wood into the fireplace and take the letter while the logs start to crackle and spit. My name is on the outside of the note, along with Sasha's. It's written in Father's hand.

I glance at my sister, but she just drops her eyes to the letter, so I unfold it.

My Dearest Daughters,

I find myself detained with essential work at the palace—I must stay here until the dire situation with our neighbours Pyots'k and Magadanskya is more stable. Do not worry; I am sure that under Queen Inessa's rule, we will achieve peace yet.

The queen has found it necessary that your mother travel to the far reaches of our realm to deal with estate management issues near the mountain pass into Pyots'k.

I will see you soon, my loves, all being well.

Your loving father

I drop into the chair on the other side of the fire. "Mother's gone."

Sasha nods. "And Father is *detained*."

I jolt upright. "Do you think he meant to warn us?"

My sister shakes her head, her expression troubled. "I can't tell. But either way, Inessa has control over both of our parents." Her shoulders slump.

The fire takes hold, flaring up and roaring in the fireplace. I lean into the warmth, putting my frozen feet on the hearth.

"Do you think we should stop?" I ask. I don't know if I want her to say yes or no.

My sister looks straight at me. "Stop hunting Anastasia? Stop fighting for our queen and our country? Stop doing the right thing?"

I smile, my heart lifting, and Sasha smiles back. Then I tell her everything that happened today, until the fire is burning low again and neither of us can keep our eyes open any more.

My boots squeak through fresh snow in the morning as I walk to the market square to meet Anatol. Before we parted last night, he told me to arrive early and to prepare to be there all day, so I'm wrapped in my warmest furs, a thickly lined *ushanka* on my head. I left Sasha fashioning a crutch for herself in the kitchen; her ankle is much less swollen now, but still barely fit to hobble on. The house was quiet, empty and cold. Neither of us talked much while we ate breakfast, both wrapped up in thoughts of our parents.

The stalls are all opening up when I arrive. A girl sweeping snow from the main pathways frowns at a boy who shakes a sack cloth off on the cobbles. Workers lay out fresh fish, fine cloth, and fruit transported in from Magadanskya.

On the far side of the square, beyond the smoke rising from a brazier, a tall figure waves at me. His dark cloak moves as he lifts his arm, the glint of a short sword just visible. I hurry over. "Nicolai."

"Valor."

He looks much brighter today, with an appointed task and his sword back in place, even if his uniform isn't. We grin at each other for a second before he remembers himself and beckons me to an awning over a shop. There, a cloaked Prince Anatol is pretending to examine the contents of the display window, his back to the slowly gathering crowd of early morning shoppers.

"Will anyone from the palace arrive this early?" I ask.

The prince shakes his head. "That's why we needed to be here right from the minute the market opens. I wasn't sure of the time, only the day. And unless Inessa has given orders changing the routine of all the kitchen staff, there'll definitely be palace servants here today."

Nicolai rests his hands on his belt. "And you and I can spot them, Valor. We both know what their uniforms look like, and with two of us patrolling the market, we should be able to find them while Prince Anatol lies low."

Anatol nods. "I'll be in this shop. The owner knows me and is loyal to my mother. He's supplied the fabric for all her gowns since she was a young girl. Bring the servants to me here. I can question them. We'll soon find out who helped Anastasia escape from the dungeon." He grabs my shoulder and shakes it slightly. "Once we know that, Nicolai has agreed to help us get that person out of the palace. We'll find out everything they know about where Anastasia's gone and what she intends to do next. I'm getting my mother back, Valor." Anatol smiles, his eyes bright with hope. A mischievous look crosses his face. "Even if you have to use that crossbow of yours again to make it happen."

He'll never let me forget the shot I took at him from the bell tower. But now it's a link between us, not a barrier.

The marketplace is huge, covering the expanse of the square, which is wider than the palace itself, so Nicolai and I divide it up into sections that we'll cover and set points where we'll meet. Anatol disappears into the shop, rolls of fabric hiding him from view, and then it's up to us.

I take a long look at the palace, as though my father might be pounding on one of the windows, trying to get my attention. He may be surrounded by plush carpets, and the guards might be wearing royal sashes and not prison tattoos, but he's a prisoner in there just as much as I was in Tyur'ma.

I turn to the nearest market stall and examine its fur mittens and *ushankas*. If I want to beat Anastasia and Inessa at their own games, I have to learn their rules. My bow can't help me now, however much I might miss its presence on my back.

I soon become adept at picking out and discarding the uniforms of servants from the other great houses, not meeting anyone's eyes or drawing attention to myself. I search for the palace uniform and screen everything else out.

I remember how the fine fabric of such a uniform felt against my own skin as I hid in the dark in the palace, watching as Anastasia took the stolen music box from its hiding place.

I move faster, winding between the stalls, drawing the collar of my furs up around my neck and pulling my earflaps down. But though I pass Nicolai three times, each time we shake our heads—the palace servants aren't here.

I'm beginning to think I should purchase something or ask Nicolai to swap routes when I see him: a kitchen boy wearing the simple cream tunic and grey furs that mark him as a palace servant. I judge him to be a little older than me, his eyes darker, almost black, but his skin is lighter than mine. He lifts a laden basket to move past a group of haggling customers, and I lunge forward and take it from his grasp.

"Here, let me help you," I say.

He opens his mouth, then frowns. Does he recognise me?

"Someone very important wishes to speak to you," I say in a low voice.

"And someone very important back at the palace will have my hide if I don't deliver this produce to the kitchen on time," he says warily, though I can tell he's intrigued.

"Better be quick, then." I turn my back, keeping firm hold of the basket, and hurry away from him.

"Hey!"

I push through the crowd as fast as I can, earning myself a few complaints but responding to none, until I'm at the door of the fabric shop. I don't wait for the kitchen boy, just open the door and spin inside. When he catches up to me and grabs for the basket, I hook my leg around and give him a swift kick so I can close the door behind us both.

He lurches into the shop and turns on me indignantly, snatching back the basket before stopping short and staring over my shoulder.

"Viktor?" Prince Anatol, concealed from the shop window by a great roll of gold brocade, lowers the hood of his cloak.

Viktor's eyes widen, and then he drops into a hasty bow. "Your Highness."

I edge towards the door, putting myself between it and Viktor. I'm not sure I trust anyone from the palace, whether they bow to Anatol or not.

When Viktor straightens, he looks from me to Anatol and back again. "You're—"

"In need of some information," I say, crossing my arms and stepping forward.

"Valor," says Anatol gently, "Viktor has worked for my mother since he was a child. Both of his parents work for her."

I open my mouth to ask what difference knowing someone for a long time makes—we all knew Anastasia, not to mention the fact that she's Anatol's own sister, but one look at his face tells me he's already thought the same thing.

"Viktor, we don't have much time," Anatol says. "All we need to know is who helped my sister escape from the palace dungeon." The prince takes a step towards Viktor and draws himself up. And even though Viktor is taller, he wilts. I've been questioned by the prince more than once myself, at Tyur'ma. I don't envy Viktor now, squirming under the commanding gaze Anatol can summon when he wants to.

The prince lifts his chin. "Do you know?"

Viktor hesitates, and then shakes his head, his eyes resting on the still-healing cut on Anatol's lip.

"Do you work for Inessa now?" I demand.

"No!" Viktor looks horrified and then worried in quick succession. "That is, I—I am loyal to the royal family. I mean to our queen. I mean, to Queen Ana!"

His confusion would be funny if it weren't so awful. He's not even sure himself where his allegiances should lie. I wonder if everyone in the city, in the whole of Demidova, feels this way too. How can we ever expect to restore order without Queen Ana?

"If you're loyal, then prove it," I say. "You must know who helped Anastasia. The staff at the palace talk, I know they do."

It's true. Sasha once told me that if she wanted to know if something was going on in the palace, she would talk to the servants. Those girls and boys are everywhere, but no one really sees them. They hear everything.

Viktor shakes his head. "I am loyal to you and your family, Prince Anatol, I swear it." He says it with conviction, but his hands are clenched tight around the handle of the basket. "I just—I don't know who helped the princess escape."

I'm about to grab whatever's at hand—fabric scissors, a loose knitting needle if need be—and tell him I know he's lying when the bell on the shop door jangles. Viktor startles so hard that he spills a ripe damson from his basket, and it splits on the polished wooden floor. Nicolai appears, closely followed by a girl wearing the same cream tunic as Viktor.

"This is Polina," Nicolai says, sounding slightly put out that I found someone first. "One of her duties is to help light the fires in the morning."

"It means I hear a lot of things, Your Highness," the girl says. She steps forward with her head up, and right away I know she wants to tell us what those things are.

Viktor looks like a cornered rabbit, but Anatol smiles. "And you're willing to tell us?" he asks.

The girl nods. "Nicolai told me what you want to know and why you want to know it. It's just—"

She stops and takes a breath. Her hands are shaking. One is smaller than the other by at least half, and she makes them both into fists and pushes them into the pockets of her tunic.

". . . you're not going to like what I have to say, Prince Anatol."

Anatol takes a slow breath. "My sister is a traitor, my mother is gone, we have a queen regent who seeks only her own glory, and the country teeters on the brink of war," he says. "There is little that I like about any of these things, and yet I must know about them."

Polina bites her lip, and she and Viktor exchange glances. He slides his basket to the floor.

"We can only hope to put any of this right if you tell us who helped the princess," I say. "Whoever it is may know something vital about the queen's whereabouts. You must see how urgent it is that we find her. She has to retake the throne. We *need* to maintain the alliance with Magadan-skya and keep Pyots'k out, and all of that is going to crumble if you don't do your duty and tell your prince what he wants to know. Do you want Saylas to invade us because Pyots'k waged war on them?"

Anatol and Nicolai both stare at me. I might be slightly offended if I weren't so surprised at myself. Words like that might come out of Sasha's mouth, but not so easily out of my own.

Polina takes a couple of breaths, and we all wait.

"I'll tell you," she says. "But you have to believe me. And you have to let us both go."

The way she says it sends a spike of worry through me. Nicolai's expression is guarded, and everyone in the room is tense.

Anatol nods. "You have my word."

Polina takes her hands out of her pockets and smooths the front of her tunic.

"It was the king."

CHAPTER 15

There's a stunned silence. It can't have been the king, but at the same time it must have been. Now I see why Viktor was so reluctant to speak.

Polina hasn't taken her eyes off Anatol.

"She's his daughter. His only daughter," she says quietly.

Anatol nods. I can't tell how he's feeling from his blank face, but I don't need to guess.

"Thank you, Polina, Viktor. You may both leave. And . . ." Anatol falters for a moment.

"Tell no one," I say, picking up Viktor's basket and pressing it into his hands.

The two servants give each other a look and then hurry from the shop. The bell over the door jingles merrily in the silence.

Anatol stares into space, so I address myself to Nicolai. "Where is the king now?"

Nicolai tears his gaze from Anatol's face to answer me. "He never leaves the palace. I hear he keeps entirely to his chambers now that Inessa . . . But even if he did know where Anastasia is—"

"Father can't have known Anastasia would take Mother," says Anatol. His cheeks are flushed, and his chest is moving up and down much too fast. Nicolai doesn't look much better.

"You don't have to do a thing," I say quickly. "If it were a servant or a guard, it would be different, but we can't interrogate the *king*. He's your father. And it's far too risky for you to try to enter the palace." I almost touch his shoulder, but I don't know whether I ought to. In the end I press my fists together. "There must be another way to find Anastasia."

Anatol's eyes are wide, fixed on a point on the floor. He shakes his head, very slightly and only to himself.

"Come on," I say, heading for the door.

"Where are we going?" asks Nicolai, hurrying after me.

"To my house." I push away the twinge of unease I feel at knowing neither Mother nor Father will be there. "We need Sasha."

Anatol doesn't ask why—he doesn't question me at all. He just submits when I go to pull his hood low over his face, and then he follows us out. I keep my eyes open for anyone trailing us and maintain a pace that leaves us all out of breath by the time we approach the house. Nicolai stands out of sight with Anatol while I sneak closer to check that Inessa doesn't have any more surprises for us. My cheeks sting as I scan for any guards, but everything is just as I left it—smoke curling into the sky from the kitchen fire, snow lying deep and untouched in drifts that almost reach the windowsills.

I take Anatol and Nicolai inside and find Sasha right where I left her at the kitchen table—with two additions.

"Valor! When we didn't hear from you, we asked Mila to get us your address. We were just talking strategy." Feliks savours that last word, grinning at me. But his face falls once we step inside and throw off our cloaks and furs.

"What's wrong?" asks Katia, her expression wary as she eyes Anatol. "Couldn't you find anyone from the palace?"

Anatol says nothing, so I tell them as we all gather around the kitchen table. I actually hear Sasha gasp when I say King Fillip helped Anastasia escape.

The others look dismayed too—not just for Anatol, but about what it means for us. Following this lead was our last hope; it was all we had left. A servant we could have bribed or cajoled or even threatened. But this is the king.

Nobody knows what to say.

My stomach rumbles. I push up from my seat at the head of the table and go to the store cupboard, then the icebox outside, stamping the snow off my boots as I come back in.

Sasha nods, giving me a small smile, and I start making a chicken broth that's soon bubbling and sending fragrant wafts of steam to cloud the windows. Katia builds the fire up high until it crackles warmth into the room, and Nicolai slices bread into hunks with a knife he weighs in his hands before he starts.

"Cut it like this," I say, trying to take the knife from him.

He holds it out of reach. "I know how to use a knife, Valor," he says with a glance at the prince.

Anatol doesn't look up from the table, even when I dig out packets of dried figs and apricots. I know they have them at the palace too—they were a gift to Father from the queen. But I know he won't mind me breaking into them on a day like today.

"Fit for a prince," says Feliks, glancing at Anatol. His fingers aren't especially clean when he picks up his spoon, but Katia just presses her lips together instead of saying anything.

I didn't realise just how hungry I was until I started eating, and everyone else must feel the same, because there's no talk for five straight minutes. I think about the last time

I ate with Sasha, Katia and Feliks by my side—in the ice hall in Tyur'ma. We had problems then too, but we always solved them. Now I'm not so sure we can.

Anatol slows, then puts down his spoon. The rest of us raise our eyes. He looks as though he's about to say something. Feliks carries on shovelling food into his mouth until Sasha nudges him.

"I don't see what more we can do," Anatol says flatly. I open my mouth, but the prince shrugs. "I'm just saying, Valor, I don't have any other ideas. I don't want to pretend that I do."

"Then let's not," says Sasha. "Let's lay everything on the table instead. If anyone has an idea, even one that sounds like it won't work, even half of one, then say it. It's how things get done. It's how committees work."

Trust my sister to see it that way. It's all new to me. I concocted the plan to break Sasha out of Tyur'ma by myself. But now, as I look around the table while Feliks's fingers inch towards the apricots, I wonder how much easier it would have been if I'd had help from the start, not just after I got into Tyur'ma.

"Well, I only know what we can't do," says Katia. "We can't go to the palace. We can't ask anyone there for help, because they're only interested in helping themselves."

Nicolai's hand drops to the table. "That's a bit harsh. You can't talk about the royal family like—"

"No, she's right," says Sasha. "Saying it nicely isn't going to make it less of a problem. None of us knows anyone else with the resources Inessa has. If she really wanted Queen Ana found, she could do it. But she doesn't."

Feliks chews rapidly and swallows. "Anatol, do you have your own Guard?" He looks to Nicolai as if he's the answer to his question.

Nicolai shakes his head. "I'm training to be part of the Queen's Guard," he says. "If—" He pulls himself up short with a quick, guilty look at Anatol. "*When* Queen Ana comes back, I'll be at her command. But until then, even though Inessa has her own Guard, we all take our orders from Inessa too. She's queen regent." He says this as though he's certain of it, but his face is a battleground.

The others keep talking and I try to listen, but something bold and unexpected is rapidly shooting up in my mind like a pine tree from the forest floor.

"How can we fight against two powerful princesses?" Katia shakes her head, her braids jostling against her shirt.

My palm smacks the table. "We pit them against each other." I shift forward to the edge of my seat.

"How?" Sasha mirrors me, a forgotten fig in her hand.

I pause for a beat. I don't think I've ever come up with anything like this before. Katia looks doubtful, but all of them are rapt, no one moving, all eyes on me.

"We do the exact opposite of what Katia said," I say. "We tell Inessa *exactly* what happened down in that cavern. Tell her Anastasia is right here in Demidova, that she wants the throne and that she'll never stop until she has it. We use the situation to our advantage and play them off each other."

Anatol's and Sasha's eyes are bright now.

"We're not going to avoid Inessa any more," I say. "In fact, I'm going to see her right now."

CHAPTER 16

My heart thumps uncomfortably loudly as Sasha and I march across the square towards one of the purple-sashed guards who now stand outside the golden gates of the palace.

Sasha's ankle is better today, but she still has to use the crutch she made. Feliks had gone to see whether Mila could find some way to get Sasha here without her having to walk. He came back with a donkey and told me not to ask where it came from, but to be assured it would be returned.

Now Feliks, Katia, Anatol and Nicolai hang back in the alley between the baker's and the florist's.

We reach the gates. They've been polished to a high shine, like the boots of the guard who frowns at us.

"We wish to speak with Queen Inessa on a matter of national importance," says Sasha, barely slowing as she makes to step past the guard. He bars our way, and we both give him our most surprised and commanding looks.

"Do you know who we are?" asks my sister, her voice all haughty disdain. The guard opens his mouth, but Sasha doesn't stop. "Perhaps, since you are new to Demidova and the palace, you do not, in which case we will forgive your impertinence. I am Sasha Raisayevna, and this is my sister, Valor. Our parents are adviser and first huntswoman to Queen Ana of Demidova, and to Queen Inessa in her stead. They're both engaged in essential work for her at this very minute."

Sasha's voice wobbles on the last sentence and her ankle gives a little, slipping on a cobble. She winces, and I grip her elbow.

"Now kindly inform the queen that we're here," I say. "She won't be pleased to hear we've been kept waiting at the gates."

The guard doesn't take his eyes off us, but he gestures to another guard within the gardens and speaks to her in a low voice. They both eye us, and my back prickles, becoming damp under my furs. Inessa has already threatened us, already sent our mother away. Father's in the palace right now. Our house is empty without them, and it feels like far too long since we were safe. I wish with all my heart that I hadn't been so difficult in the Magadanskyan palace. I was spoiled and bored, when all Mother did was worry about me and love me. I start to think this is all too risky, but just as I turn to Sasha, she steps forward. We've been beckoned inside.

The palace gates swing open and closed, golden and curlicued, a hundred times more beautiful than anything at Tyur'ma. But the same trapped feeling surfaces nonetheless. I stay close to Sasha, our arms touching—partly to help her stand straight, and partly because my heart is still hammering.

We have to wait again at the palace doors while a sharp-eyed adviser listens to the guard's whispered message. I hold my breath, straining to hear, but I can't pick up a word. The adviser looks us up and down and then plasters on a cold smile. "I'm afraid Queen Inessa is busy with matters of state, and expects to be so for the remainder of the day."

"She'll want to hear what we have to say," says Sasha.

"It's a matter of national security," I add, staring straight back at the adviser. Her dark hair is coiled around her head in hundreds of braids.

"Perhaps you can convey your message to me, and I can be the judge of that. I'll be happy to pass the information to our queen if, as you say, it is so important."

I square my shoulders. They feel bare without a bow, but Sasha said it wouldn't have been appropriate to bring one. I'm beginning to think it would have done very nicely.

"This is private information, fit only for the queen's ears," I say.

The adviser's nostrils flare at the slight.

I push it further. "It's regarding Princess Anastasia."

Sasha stiffens, and I wonder if I've said the wrong thing, but the adviser's face changes at once. I've definitely got her attention now. She steps back, so I link arms with my sister and, keeping my head held up straight, we walk right into the palace as though we own the place.

"Wait here," says the adviser. I can tell she's trying not to run as she hurries across the polished mosaic of the floor and disappears down a corridor. Sasha swallows, and it seems very loud in the great hall. I want to ask if she still thinks we're doing the right thing, but I feel like we're being watched. We probably are.

We stand in silence for a few minutes before the adviser reappears and beckons us down the corridor with a sour look. We follow her deep into the palace, past tapestries and paintings and endless closed doors, until we reach a final set of doors that the adviser sweeps open. Opposite us, framed by a large window, stands Queen Inessa. My eyes are drawn straight to the view outside. Squarely in the middle of the mountain vista is Tyur'ma.

I'm pulled right back there, back to the chains and the cells and the towering, tattooed Peacekeepers. To the hunger and the blisters on my hands from working in the mine.

To Warden Kirov and her punishments—the ice dome that nearly killed Sasha. And to the constant fear that even if my sister survived the prison, I wouldn't be able to rescue her.

Sasha touches my hand, and I'm back in the warm palace, plush carpet under my boots and the faint smell of pollen on the air from hothouse flowers that don't grow anywhere else in Demidova.

I would love nothing more than to rush across the room and shake the composed look off our new queen's face. But that's what she wants. Standing there, in this particular room—it's hardly accidental. I think about Inessa being slung into a cell like the one Sasha was kept in. I think about me slamming the door, and the look on her face when she realises that she should never have threatened my family.

"We've come with new information about the traitor Princess Anastasia," I say. "In fact"—I actually lower myself on to one knee—"I've personally come to apologise for having her in my grasp and letting her get away."

Sasha sinks down next to me, and I pick that moment to raise my lowered eyes. Relief and pleasure mingle on the queen's face, and she doesn't quite manage to wipe them away before we lock gazes. I look down at the carpet again. "Of course, we knew you would want to know right away what she said when we encountered her, and what we know about where Queen Ana is."

"Of course I do," says Inessa. "It is my sworn duty to find Queen Ana and to apprehend the criminal princess. Pray, where did you come upon her, and what was it Princess Anastasia said?"

Sasha squeezes my hand again. She hears the note of greed in the queen regent's voice. Inessa is just as eager for Anastasia never to be found again as I thought she would be.

"We were underneath the library in a secret cavern, and she said . . ." I pause for effect. Queen Inessa steps forward, and then recalls herself.

I take a breath. "She said she's intent on having the throne, that it's hers by right and that she won't stop until she's taken it back from the nasty, self-serving, manipulative, conniving usurper who now sullies it."

Inessa takes in a little breath, and Sasha pinches my back. I might have gone a little overboard. But I'm sure Anastasia might very well say those things if she were here.

My sister clears her throat. "We thought that keeping any detail of this from you would not be to our family's benefit. We want you to know that we are wholly ready to cooperate. Valor and I understand exactly what's at stake. Is . . . is our father still busy with his work here at the palace?"

"Yes, yes," says the queen dismissively. "Now tell me everything about where you found Anastasia and where you think she went."

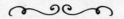

A short while later, we're making our way back down through the palace gardens to the golden gates, having answered all of Inessa's questions about the cavern and the tunnel and the boat that carried the princess away with the queen trapped on board. She evaded or ignored Sasha's further mentions of Father and Mother, and I didn't trust myself to open my mouth again, even though words burned in my throat.

As the guard at the gate lets us out and we walk across the square, I catch a glimpse of Feliks with two other boys. He pushes off the wall he's been leaning against and touches his fingers to his *ushanka* in a subtle salute. I nod back. Katia's harder to spot, but eventually I see her on the other side of the square. She's tucked her pale braids into her furs, and though her skin is still lighter than everyone else's, with her hair hidden she isn't so noticeable. I nod at her too.

It's time to see if the rest of my plan will work—if we'll get the results I'm hoping for.

Once we've blended into the throng of people going about their business, Sasha and I make a sharp left. We're going to meet Anatol and Nicolai at the back of the palace. Sasha starts to limp even with the use of her crutch. I hope Nicolai's been able to get the horses.

I'm all nerves, constantly sweeping my gaze around us by the time I see Nicolai in his dark cloak. He beckons us, and I see four horses, all saddled, all stamping and snorting. They're standing under the awning of a blacksmith's forge.

Sasha casts a worried look at Anatol, who has hold of two of the horses' bridles.

"We paid the blacksmith," says Anatol. "We had to—this place has the perfect view." He nods over our shoulders, and I turn to see that the palace stables are right in our sights.

I help Sasha over to a worn wooden bench, and she sighs and eases her leg out in front of her as I lower her on to it.

I take up a position next to Anatol and Nicolai, whose eyes are trained on the stables.

A few minutes later, I begin to doubt my plan, and the seconds stretch out, taking my nerves with them. Our horses start to get restless, but then there's a commotion at the palace. Stableboys come running with saddles and other tack. Horses are readied and led outside, their hooves clopping on the swept cobbles. Sasha said that if Inessa sent spies out, those leaving on horseback would depart from the back of the palace, and those on foot would leave through the front. Neither Katia nor Feliks can ride, so they're watching the golden gates. It seems as though my idea is working: Inessa's taken the bait, and her spies are mobilising.

I had hoped that Inessa would react to the news about Anastasia this way, but it was an incredibly risky strategy. We need Inessa's resources, but we also need to find Anastasia and Queen Ana before Inessa does. I have to be the one to capture Anastasia and rescue the queen—otherwise, who knows what Inessa will do with them? I don't trust her not to imprison the queen along with Anastasia. Or maybe she would arrange for some kind of accident to befall the queen so she could keep the throne for herself. I don't know how deep and twisted her ambition is. I don't dare to dwell too long on it.

My blood fizzes. "Ready?"

Anatol and Nicolai nod, and I help Sasha mount one of the horses. The animals pick up on our excitement, tossing their heads and stepping back and forth, but we hold them back. It's imperative that the queen's spies don't know we intend to follow them.

The spies make their exit from the stables and head out through the gates. There are five of them, their horses unmarked by palace livery, their cloaks plain and dark, the hoods pulled low over their faces. With only four of us, we'll have to let one of them go.

There's virtually no one around this side of the palace. The streets are quiet, but the spies still keep a measured pace, drawing no attention to themselves. We follow at a distance, keeping the horses reined in single file, until the five riders reach a wide crossroads. I hold up my hand to let the others know to stop. There's a water trough nearby, and I lead our party to it, pretending the horses need to drink.

One spy heads down the main road that leads out of the city. Nicolai nods at me, then takes off after her. One heads towards Tyur'ma. "Hold back," I say to Anatol. Maybe someone at the prison has information, but my instincts tell me not this time, and I can't afford to send one of us towards a likely dead end. The prince follows the next spy, my sister the one after that.

Sasha gives me a tense smile as she canters past. "You always put yourself last. You just can't bear not to see what happens in the end, can you!" Her words trail off, drifting on the air, but I hear the teasing note in them.

I allow myself to smile after my sister for a second, and then I spur my horse and take off after the last spy.

CHAPTER 17

The spy's horse picks its way swiftly through the streets on neat hooves, its rider's cloak flowing back along the horse's brown satin flanks. I follow a long way behind, hoping my own mount's footfalls are lost in the noise made by the passing carts and laden donkeys in the city.

Snow starts to fall, and I'm grateful to it for muffling my horse's steps, but I'm so focused on not losing sight of my spy that I don't take notice of my surroundings. When she stops and dismounts, I finally look up and see where we are—the Great Library.

I hang back, my horse shaking its head and twitching its ears to flick away the thick snowfall, but there are no guards outside the library today. They must have conducted their search and let the librarians resume normal service—either that, or Inessa's ordered them away, not caring for them to find any evidence of the true queen.

I dismount and hitch my horse to the nearest post. A boy smaller than Feliks hovers, having seen me pull up. I rummage in my pocket for a coin and toss it to him as I stride through the snow, glad of the excuse to pull my furs around me and keep my head down.

The spy flits up the steps of the library. I wait for as long as I can force myself to after the doors close behind her, then run up the steps two at a time. Inside, I shake melting flakes from my clothes. I just catch a glimpse of a fast-moving figure ascending the staircase, and then she's gone. I follow on hunter's feet. She passes a librarian and doesn't even acknowledge the man. She knows exactly where she's going, neither slowing nor turning around.

We go all the way to the top of the building, and I duck behind a marble bust on a tall pillar when she reaches the same doors Anatol, Katia, Nicolai, Feliks and I passed through yesterday. Once she's stepped into the genealogy room and closed the doors, I creep forward and put my ear to the carved wood. Nothing. Is she looking for the secret passageway we discovered—or is there something in the room we missed when we were here?

I ease the door open, my muscles tensed, ready to take off if I'm discovered. But as I gradually pull the door open wider, I realise the room is empty. I straighten and, with a quick glance behind me, step into the room and stride to the far end. The clock—the secret door—is ajar.

The second time around, I know not to touch anything, and I go faster as I wind down the stairs to the cavern. I wonder how the spy knows to avoid the traps that caught us. Maybe the secrets of the royal family aren't as secret as Anatol thinks.

At the entrance to the cavern, I peek into the darkness. I don't even see the spy until she moves, and then I freeze—she's right in front of me. I hold my breath until my pulse pounds, but her back is to me, hands on her hips as she surveys the space. Only one torch burns—she must have lit it—and it throws just the barest hint of light into the far-thest reaches of the cave, where I know the cell is.

She lifts the torch and moves to the edge of the water. I stay hidden, watching her pause, work out the bridge and then slowly make her way across. She goes a little way down the tunnel I helplessly watched Anastasia escape through, and as the flare of the torch gets smaller and smaller, I step out into the cavern itself.

The torch's movement changes. I halt and squint into the darkness to be sure I'm right. It's coming back towards me. I slip into the passageway, backing up farther and far-ther until I'm certain—the spy discovered no more than I did. She's leaving.

I bolt up the stairs, knowing I have to get out of the genealogy room before I'm discovered. If Inessa finds out I orchestrated this whole situation, my father will pay the price. My stomach twists as I realise what a risk I've taken, what a risk I've forced my sister and the others to take. Inessa could put every one of us back in Tyur'ma. Or she could do something worse.

The stairs curl upwards in a tight spiral. My legs churn, and my hand scrapes along the rough stone until I burst out from the clock into the room and run straight for the door. At the last second I decide I won't make it and throw myself behind a glass case full of glittering jewels. I realise that I'm not fully hidden, but there's no time. The clock swings open, and the black-cloaked spy strides out. She has a long, straight nose and eyes as watchful as a mountain cat's. She flicks the hood of her cloak over her dark braids as she closes the clock door.

I try to slow my breathing, but it only rushes in my ears. I squeeze my eyes shut, waiting for the banging in my chest to give me away. Seconds pass, and I blink. The spy is gone. I should have kept my eyes open.

But the room is quiet. She can't have seen me. I push to my feet and run for the door, slipping out into the hallway just in time to see the hem of the spy's cloak disappear around a corner in the direction of the map room.

"Can I help you?" The tone is stern, and I straighten and spin around.

"I—I'm looking for the map room," I say.

The librarian eyes me sharply. Everyone in the city is suspicious now that Queen Ana has disappeared. That probably goes double for people who work in the place she disappeared from. The last thing I need is for anyone to call the Guard.

The librarian frowns at me, and then gives me directions I barely hear and don't actually need. I just nod, and when she seems intent on watching me, I head for the map room, walking as slowly as I can.

The door stands open and the spy is gone, but there are two scholars in the room—plus the librarian outside—so I enter and walk straight to a window. The spy's horse is gone. I press my face to the glass and crane my neck to look both ways down the street, but there's no trace. I've lost her. My horse is still hitched, though the boy I paid to watch it has deserted his post. I'd better get down there quickly.

"What is the meaning of all of these intrusions?" One of the scholars glares at me, her foot tapping impatiently.

I turn to her. "All of these . . . ?" The spy. The spy was in here.

"Why are you staring, girl? What do you want?"

"I want the same thing the woman who was in here before did," I say.

The scholar tuts and waves her arm at one corner of the room, then pulls her candle closer and presses her nose to the map she's studying.

I move to the corner she pointed out. A dull glass case positioned there holds rolled maps stuffed inside seemingly at random, making the whole thing look like a honeycomb

I once pulled down from a tree in the garden at home. It broke on the grass and spat out a swirl of bees that had me sprinting for the house while Sasha flung the door open and yelled for me to run.

One map, though—one map is sticking out farther than the others, as though it was replaced in a hurry. I pull it out, brush a cobweb away and unfurl the yellowed, powdery parchment. Faded brown ink outlines the familiar lands of the realm—including the flat, featureless land labelled only "Saylas"—but this map is so old that the Demidovan forests are double the size they are today, spreading over what is now farmland. The city is tiny, and though the mountains look exactly the same, the rivers look different somehow.

I stare at it, trying to fathom the reason the spy picked this particular map. I trace the river that runs through the valley outside the city with my finger, following its path through Demidova and out to the sea. There's another river in the lands beyond the mountains; the map shows it running through Pyots'k, but then it just stops. It must be incomplete. Rivers don't just stop.

I stand up straighter. *Rivers don't just stop. But maybe they disappear underground.* Maybe whoever made this map didn't know where this river went. Maybe they had no way of finding out.

I run to the table and lay the map in my hands next to an up-to-date map of Demidova. Then I run back to the stack of ancient maps and pull them out one by one to unfurl them and run my fingers along the faded blue lines of rivers.

The scholar tuts at me again, but I ignore her, even though both the table and the floor are covered now. Some of the maps are so old that I can't read the writing, and on some the countries I know are called different names altogether.

I stand back, and then when I can't see everything at once, I clamber up on to a chair.

"Young lady, if you don't desist at once, I am going to call for assistance," the scholar says.

"Sorry," I say, but I don't stop, and I don't care. Back in the cavern, we decided that the river simply led to the sea, and that we had no chance of catching Anastasia or finding anything more to help us.

But we were wrong.

We were looking in the wrong direction—thinking only about were the river went, and not where it came from. Now I see, as I stand and survey the maps, that the river came from Pyots'k. It all started there. Why would Anastasia need to use a river that comes through Pyots'k to Demidova?

The scholar is talking to me again, but I ignore her. I'm thinking about what Anastasia said back in the cavern— that she still wants the throne, and that she'll have it. She always intended to ally with Pyots'k, and she still means to. If they launch their ships from our harbours, if their fleet wins the war they aim to start, they'll put Anastasia on the Demidovan throne in return.

I jump down from the chair just as the irate scholar swings open the door to the map room. Behind her is the librarian. I run past them both, and they shout after me. I'm halfway down the stairs, going too fast for my own feet, before I realise the full extent of what's happening.

I have to get to the others. We have to return to that tunnel and follow it to its end.

We have to see what Anastasia's been secretly bringing in on that river from Pyots'k.

CHAPTER 18

"Hurry up!" I call over my shoulder for the tenth time. I've been desperate to get back here since the moment I burst out of the Great Library into fresh knee-deep snow and rode hard back home.

Anatol, Katia, Sasha, Feliks and Nicolai follow me into the tunnel that carries the river from Pyots'k, through the cavern in Demidova, and out to the sea. I grudgingly admit to myself that Sasha and Katia were right to make us wait until morning to do this as I lead them into the dark of the tunnel with a freshly lit torch, dry furs and a borrowed crossbow at my back.

"Careful." I point out a stone underfoot that's slick with moss. The tunnel walls are curved stone, and the path beside the river is narrow. We have to walk single file, our torches flaring out over the black water. My bow is wedged at an angle, digging into my back.

"How long is this tunnel, anyway?" Feliks's voice echoes.

I think back to the maps, trying to judge the distance. "We'll have to walk for two hours." I secretly wonder whether it might be more, but Sasha insisted she come along, and her ankle is still sore, so I don't want to say it aloud.

Behind me, Anatol is silent. When I glance back, his face is taut in the orange torchlight. I go as fast as I can—almost a breakneck speed on the treacherous stones of the path—but he's hot on my heels the whole way, the heat from his torch warming my hand if I slow at all.

We walk a long way like that, no one saying anything, until Sasha calls out, "Can we rest? Just for a minute?"

It's not until I look back again that I see how far behind the others are. I look to Anatol, and he nods.

"OK," I call back. "For a few minutes."

We stop where we are and I crouch to rest my back against the damp wall. Anatol does the same, his torch spitting as an errant drop of moisture falls on it. The flickering light throws shadows under his eyes, but they only add to those that are already there.

"We'll find the queen," I say in a low voice. "There's more to this tunnel than there seems, I know it."

"She doesn't know," he says, his voice small and fragile.

"What?"

"My mother. She doesn't know what Father's done, and how Inessa's betrayed her too, on top of Anastasia." He rubs his hand over his face, pressing too hard. "If we ever do find her, I'll have to tell her what they've done."

"She'll still have you," I say, because I don't know what else I *can* say.

"You don't understand," he says in a louder voice. "Everyone has betrayed us, and she's not here. I don't . . . I don't have anyone." He sighs and slumps to the ground.

I think about my parents—kept from us, but not gone. They've never let Sasha and me down, but I know how much it hurts to be away from them, to know they're worrying about us. I think about Sasha too, how she's plunged deeper and deeper into Father's world since she got out of Tyur'ma. How she's moved farther away from *my* world. We've had to push the rift aside, often, since we returned to Demidova, but her not telling me about Anatol's banishment is like a hot ember inside me that won't go out. I've dulled it—she's done nothing but help since Queen Ana gave us our tasks—but I still can't extinguish it, not entirely.

"I'm sorry," I say to Anatol. "But you have all of us. We're here with you."

"Katia and Feliks hate me. They think I'm a spoiled prince who endangered the thieves' network. Nicolai is *paid* to be near me. Sasha's loyalty lies above all with my mother, and—"

"Don't you dare," I say sharply. "Don't you dare tell me why I'm here. Katia and Feliks were annoyed with you over something you *did*. It doesn't mean they hate you. Say you're sorry and mean it. They won't hold it against you. Nicolai would be *offended* if he heard you say that about him, so you'd better count yourself lucky that I won't tell. My sister is doing this for you, and for me, and for the entire country, because *that's* what she cares about, and *I'm* here because I'm your friend and I want to put things right just as much as you do. I have just as much to lose, so—"

"Valor?"

"What?"

"I'm sorry. And I mean it."

I let out a breath and bump his shoulder with mine.

He sighs deeply. "You're right about Nicolai too. I shouldn't have said that. He's the first in his family to receive an apprenticeship, you know. I couldn't have picked anyone better than him when I chose who to send into Tyur'ma."

I twist to face the prince. He's never talked about this before. And come to think of it, neither has Nicolai.

"When I realised I needed a spy, I went to the training grounds under the pretext of taking a royal interest, and out of all the apprentices, Nicolai caught my eye. I asked the master about him, and he told me Nicolai had plans to work his way up through the ranks. I could see how determined he was, and how loyal to my family. His own family staunchly supports my mother. They think the world of him for dedicating himself to the Guard."

Anatol looks past me to where the others sit farther down the tunnel. "I really am sorry I risked the thieves' network by sending that message to Nicolai. I . . . felt like I'd lost everyone else, Valor. But I knew Nicolai would never let me down."

I nod. "Feliks and Katia understand. They know what it is to miss family. They know about loyalty."

Anatol manages a small smile. "I can tell. You know, Nicolai sends every coin he earns home for his younger brother. He says the Guard gives him everything he needs, so he doesn't want the money for himself."

Down the tunnel, Katia gets to her feet.

I nudge Anatol. "Come on. Let's go. I've had enough of being in the dark."

He nods, and I call to Sasha and pick up the pace again, thankful for the sturdy treads on the soles of my boots. We fall into silence, with only the occasional hollow drip from the roof of the tunnel into the water beside us and the shuffle and echo of our footsteps to keep us company. The path widens in places, and the roof lowers in others so much that we're forced to crouch. For one stretch we walk hunched over for so long that I can barely stand it. The hilt of Nicolai's sword scrapes the rocks more than once, setting my teeth on edge. When we eventually straighten again, everyone but little Feliks sighs in relief.

I catch movement among the shadows. A rat darts past me, and I suck in a breath through my teeth. I spin to see it scurry over Katia's foot. She gasps and drops her torch. The light flares over the dark water for a split second, and then blinks out with a hiss.

"How much farther do you think we have to go?" Nicolai asks.

I thought I saw a faint circle of light ahead before the rat distracted me, but I don't answer him. Instead I hold my torch high, peering back the way we came.

"What is it?" Sasha asks.

"Valor?" Anatol joins me, his torch adding to the light my own casts.

I squint until my eyes smart. Something in my gut, something I thought I saw in the brief light of the fall of Katia's torch, has all my senses on high alert. I screw up my eyes in frustration at not being able to see into the thick blackness down the tunnel.

"Nothing," I say. "It's nothing."

Anatol stares for a few seconds longer. Sasha touches my arm.

"I'm just on edge," I say. "I want us to find . . . *something*." I shake my head. I can't be any clearer than that. No one questioned the decision to do this, but now that we've been walking for at least two hours, and maybe more, all based on an old map and a feeling I had, I'm beginning to wonder if I've done the right thing.

Sasha touches my shoulder and nods ahead of us. "We'll find out soon enough. Look."

I turn back the way we were heading, and see that there's definitely a patch of light ahead.

"Come on, Valor; we're almost there," says Feliks.

I take up my position at the head of the line again. We walk for a long time, the light getting brighter only by tiny increments, until it gradually becomes enough that we can douse our torches. We tuck them away against the wall of the tunnel for later. Sasha looks a little pained, and everyone blinks after such a long time underground. I hadn't realised my chest was so tight, but I feel like I can breathe easier the closer we get to the light.

The smell of the sea drifts into the air, and the river gets wider. We no longer have to walk single file, and the smooth path starts to break into rougher rock beneath our boots.

"This is it," says Anatol beside me. His face is expectant—wary and worried and hopeful all at once.

I hope for his sake that this isn't another dead end.

A faint sound comes from outside the tunnel, and we all pause. It comes again, far away but unmistakable—a man's voice. We're almost at the tunnel's exit now, and the river pulses forward and out into the open air. I motion for the others to fall in behind me as we reach the end, but as we see what lies in front of us, we all just stand and stare. There's no room for thought of anything else.

The river rushes straight into the middle of a tightly curved horseshoe bay. Jagged black cliffs hem it in on either side. The odd stunted pine tree weighed down with snow juts from the rocks high above us. On the ground ahead, slick black rock shows through the snow. But it's what's out on the storm-grey water that renders us all silent and horrorstruck.

Tossing on the choppy waves is a warship, its mast high, dark sails unfurled, cannons showing through the rows of portholes lining the side of the ship. Beyond it is another, identical to the first, and beyond that another and another—a whole fleet of warships, ready to launch.

CHAPTER 19

I feel my knees start to give and reach out for the rock. On either side of the river, smaller boats are moored, and on the ground beside them lie saws and hammers and great stacks of felled trees, giant coils of rope, planks of wood and huge barrels.

The underground river from Pyots'k is only a trickle in places, barely big enough for barges, but certainly big enough to carry tools for shipbuilding. Anastasia has used it to smuggle in the materials to do . . . *this*.

"They must have been working at this for weeks—months, even." Prince Anatol's voice is faint. All I can do is nod.

Beside me, Sasha's hand is pressed over her mouth. "We must go back. Someone has to tell Father, get him to sound the alarm. We have to stop them."

Feliks's eyes are wide, staring at my sister. "Pyots'k is going to war?"

She nods. "Queen Ana would never have let them use our harbours to launch their fleet, but they're doing it anyway."

"The sails are all unfurled." Katia stands behind me, worry etched all over her face as she looks out to sea.

Nicolai nods his agreement. "It's too late. They're launching now."

"Then we must launch Demidova's fleet against them," says Sasha.

Anatol and I whip around to face her at the same time.

"That's an act of war," I say.

But even as I say it, we all know there's no other way to stop the Pyots'kan fleet now—Katia's right; the sails are set.

"It's not too late," says Feliks. "We can run back." He looks doubtfully at my sister. "Well, those who can run will run, and the rest—"

I step forward with a gasp that cuts Feliks off. Little figures run around on the ships, some clinging to the rigging, some working on the sails or on the decks. On the ship closest to us, anchored before all the others that spread like a plague over the water, is a small figure whose long dark hair whips in the breeze. She stands at the side of the ship, a telescope held to one eye, pointing straight at us.

"Anastasia!" I say.

Anatol steps forward, his body instantly rigid. "Then Mother is here. We can't go back. We must rescue her."

"But the ships—" says Katia.

"Some of us must stay, and some must go back." I look at my sister. We all blurt out ideas, everyone on the verge of panic. Anatol wants to stay, and it's clear from the pained look on Sasha's face and the way she's keeping her weight on her good ankle that she can neither run back nor run forward.

I tear my gaze away from Anastasia and the crew members who pile into a smaller boat as it's lowered into the water and turn to my friends.

"Feliks, Katia, you have to get to my father. You need to—"

From the gloom of the tunnel behind us step six cloaked people, every one of them armed.

The six of them span the width of the tunnel in a V, daggers glinting in their hands. At the head is a figure in a dark cloak who steps forward.

"You," I say.

Facing me is the spy I followed into the Great Library, and she's flanked by Inessa's other spies. Her hard gaze settles on me. I was seen after all—seen and followed. Inessa has beaten us at our own game, and I've led her spies straight here.

"I thought I'd planned everything." The words come out of me unbidden.

A nervous titter of a laugh comes from inside the tunnel. "Not carefully enough," Inessa says as she steps into the light, her usual beautiful dress exchanged for black boots and a cloak. She walks around her spies until she stands just behind the leader, whom she peers around. She looks over my shoulder at the scene in the harbour and smiles. "My, what a predicament you find yourself in."

I glance behind me. Nicolai's hand is on his sword, but he hasn't moved, his face twisted in indecision. Beyond him, Anastasia's rowing boat nears the shore.

Inessa's laugh bubbles up again. "You are a picture," she says. "Stuck between sea and stone—a rock and a hard place indeed. What are you going to do now, Valor?"

I tilt my chin up. "What are *you* going to do, Inessa? Anastasia's helping Pyots'k wage their war. What do you think she asked for in return? She wants the Demidovan throne, and she kidnapped her own mother to get it. Do you think for a moment that she'll stop just because you hold the seat now? If I were you, I'd be running back to the palace to sound the alarm, because once those warships reach Say-las and start their raids, what do you think will happen?"

Sasha steps up next to me. "Why do you think Queen Ana wanted so badly to prevent this very thing from happening? She wanted peace, not for Demidova to be caught up between Pyots'k and a revengeful invading army. Our lands lie between the two—there is no way for you to keep your throne and the peace unless we stop this fleet from launching."

Inessa titters again. "What makes you think I want the throne of Demidova?"

She touches the shoulder of the spy in front of her, who flicks her cloak aside and draws a second dagger. All the others follow suit. Feliks sucks in a breath, and I edge closer to Sasha.

Behind us I can hear Anastasia's crew making their way up the rocks, and my heartbeat accelerates until I just want to run. Sasha's fingers reach for mine, and I grasp her hand. Nicolai has a sword and I have my crossbow, but everyone else is unarmed—unarmed and outnumbered and surrounded. Feliks and Katia press close behind, Anatol and Nicolai on either side.

Inessa claps her hands. "Oh, look how close you all are. Like a pack of curs."

The spy in front of her raises both daggers.

I pull my bow from my back and aim it at Inessa. She lets out a noise and cowers behind the spy. Three of Inessa's spies advance. Nicolai's sword rings as he pulls it from its scabbard.

"Now, now, Valor, when *will* you learn to play nicely with others?"

I take a few tiny steps back and edge to the side, Sasha and the others turning with me. Anastasia stands with her crew behind her and smiles her cat-that-got-the-cream smile. But it's not aimed at me. Not at any of us.

"Cousin." She nods to Inessa, one hand at her waistband, her shoulders thrown back and her hair blowing unbraided in the breeze.

"Dearest cousin," Inessa returns, a self-satisfied smile mirrored on her face as she peeks out from behind her human shield.

They're not pitted against each other at all.

They're working together.

I heartily wish that I had more than one bolt in my crossbow.

"I must say, cousin," says Inessa, "you were right about Valor's face when she gets caught. It's worth the hours I've spent trekking through this tunnel just for that alone."

Anastasia laughs. "I'm glad you enjoy it. But of course it will pale into insignificance next to your real reward."

Inessa's high-pitched laugh flits out again, as though we're all at court and not watching as the final preparations are made to launch the Pyots'kan fleet.

"What reward?" I ask, at the very same time Anatol says, "Where is Mother?"

Inessa and Anastasia share a delighted glance that makes my heart sink even more.

I aim my bow at Anastasia, and Anatol takes half a step forward, then bites his lip, looking from me to his sister and back again.

Anastasia smiles. "You'll never find out where the *ex*-queen is if you harm me, Valor. And that really is the very best part of all this. Inessa's done a fine job of keeping you busy running around the city looking for Queen Ana. You and your precious family have been distracted, wouldn't you say? We've been building this for weeks." She sweeps her arm back over the bay, full as it is with dark sails. "I'll have the throne of Demidova, just like I told you I would. And once the Pyots'kan fleet returns victorious, we'll take Magadanskya and put Inessa on their throne."

"You can't," says Sasha, breathing hard. "It won't work."

"They only have a steward," says Inessa. "Lady Olegevna has no real claim. *I'm* of royal lineage."

"You're fourth in line and a usurper," says Anatol hotly.

She tilts her head up. "Anastasia explained it all perfectly, and I would think that *you* of all people would understand, Anatol. I'm fourth in line, and not even the first daughter in my own family. How would I ever have anything if I didn't take it for myself? But look where I am now, thanks to your sister. I'm currently your queen, and I think you should try to remember it."

"My *mother* is my queen, and everyone else's." He's furious now, his grey eyes full of fire and his jaw set. "Where is she? Release her at once." He pushes forward and then straightens, frozen. Inessa's spy presses her dagger into the back of his cloak.

"Control yourself. She isn't even here," says Anastasia.

Inessa lets out a loud, dramatic sigh. "I made her promise that Aunt Ana wouldn't be harmed, Anatol. I do care for her. I wouldn't let anything happen to her."

Anastasia's face flashes with barely concealed annoyance at her cousin.

I grip my crossbow tight, still pointing it at her.

Anastasia's attention returns to me. "I know what you're thinking, Valor. We've been here before, haven't we?" She pouts mockingly. "Now you won't believe me. You'll think I have her hidden on one of my ships. But that's exactly why I wanted you here, far, far away from the mountain pass. So far, in fact, that you have no hope of getting there before Queen Ana is handed over to Queen Lidiya of Pyots'k."

"Why would you—" I open my mouth before I stop to think. Sasha makes a little noise that tells me she worked it out before I did.

A gloating, triumphant smile spreads across Anastasia's face. "Come on, Valor. I know that between the two of you, Sasha got what brains there were, but you can figure out why I did this, can't you?"

Feliks tenses, his hands curling into fists. I stick my elbow out and press it against his shoulder.

Anastasia wanted Queen Ana elsewhere while her little puppet Inessa made sure I was here. If Inessa hadn't trapped us, we could make it back to the city and at least try to launch the Demidovan fleet against Anastasia and

Pyots'k, *or* we could head to the mountain pass to try to rescue Queen Ana before she's forced through it into Pyots'k and is lost.

I can't do both.

"There we go. The coin has finally dropped." Anastasia laughs. "This is for your own good, Valor—so you see you can never cross me and get away with it. I've covered every outcome. I've thought of *everything*."

She's right. It makes me sick, but she's right. Even if we weren't being held at knifepoint, even if we were free this second to rush away from here, which way would we go? We'd have to go back to the city and find Father. Only he would have any chance of making the military leaders listen.

But then what about Queen Ana?

"Face it," says Anastasia. "There's nothing left for you to do but watch."

She turns towards the fleet, raises her arm up high and brings it down sharply in an arc. Glints of light, like sun reflecting off glass, wink out on each ship. Someone on each of them was watching this scene with a telescope.

She looks at me over her shoulder. "In case you can't work it out, that was the signal to raise the anchors." This is it. The fleet is about to leave, and I should have done something about it before Anastasia could ever give that signal. Desperation rises in me like a tide. I lunge forward and grab for Anastasia. I catch her around the neck and drag her back against me, pressing my crossbow into the hollow above her left collarbone. Then I swing her around so we're facing both Anastasia's crew and Inessa and her spies.

"If anyone moves, I'll shoot her," I say.

Inessa lets out a squeak.

"Don't listen to her—she won't do it," snaps Anastasia. "Help me."

Nicolai raises his sword against the spies and backs up so he's between them and me. But on the other side, Anastasia's crew shifts, eyeing one another. I don't have much time.

"You'll be very sorry if you *don't* listen to her." Sasha steps to my other side, and we all start edging away, out on to the rocks that line the bay. "Do you know who she is? Do you know what she's done? This is Valor Raisayevna, and she escaped from Tyur'ma."

The crew members look at one another, and a couple of them mutter something.

"She's an excellent shot even at exceptional distances, so make no mistake: she would *not* miss or hesitate." Sasha sounds so undeniably certain. "And what's more, she's my sister, and she won't ever give up, so you'd better stay *back*."

My heart swells even though my hand is shaking. I dig the point of my bolt into Anastasia's neck until she yelps, and we all continue walking backwards, my arm tight around Anastasia, my feet feeling their way behind me on the rocks.

"Where are we going?" hisses Katia.

I don't know. We can't get back down the tunnel now, and we'd never get away if we tried. I twist around, trying to see a way out.

Anastasia shakes under my arm. I hold her tighter, but she's not shaking from fear. She's not even trying to get away.

She's laughing.

The others are looking around now too, scouring the bay for an escape route. We keep moving back towards the cliff, but that's all there are: cliffs. All the way around the bay. The only way in or out is the tunnel, which is why this was the perfect secluded spot in which to build a fleet. Anastasia's right— she's thought of everything.

But Sasha's right too—I am Valor Raisayevna. And I escaped from Tyur'ma.

"Up," I say.

Nicolai turns to look at me and lowers his sword for a moment. Anastasia wrenches herself away from me, and though my finger is on the crossbow's trigger, I hesitate. I wait a second too long, and she's gone from my grasp.

"Run!" shouts Anatol. Feliks doesn't need to be told twice. He shoots away like a mountain goat over the rocks to the base of the cliff. I sling the crossbow on to my back, grab Sasha's hand, and we follow Feliks, dashing as fast as we dare. Behind us the spies and the crew rush forward.

I look up as I run. The cliffs cut jagged black lines through a white sky. My heart leaps into my throat, the bitter taste of fear in my mouth. But I hurl myself at the rocks and start climbing after Feliks. I scramble up until I reach the cliff face.

I throw a frantic glance over my shoulder. The spies are close; the crew is behind them; and Anastasia and Inessa stand together, their cloaks snapping in the wind. Inessa wrings her hands, and Anastasia gives her an unmistakable look of scorn.

"Climb!" I'm not sure if I'm entreating the others or myself.

Nicolai sheathes his sword, and Sasha grits her teeth. I can't see Anatol or Katia, but I know that if I keep checking on them, I'll do so at the risk of losing my own grip. This is something each of us will have to do alone.

I step up, find a handhold and pull, pressing my cheek to the cold rock in front of me. Up, up I go, until I can take it no longer and have to look back to see who's following us. The Pyots'kan crew members have returned to Anastasia. They're heading back to the ships.

Already the ground is far away. A wave of dizziness hits me, and I have to cling there, unmoving, for long seconds.

"Valor, keep going." It's Feliks's voice, coming from above me somewhere.

I reach up, then move my feet to another foothold.

I pull harder, climb faster. I want Anastasia to know that when I stop this—and I *will* stop this—it was me who did it.

My breath comes in laboured gasps, and my fingers start to cramp and go numb. I see a ledge above me to my right, and I focus every ounce of energy I have left on reaching it. The pain in my hands increases, and the whole world narrows to that one ledge. I can't see anything else, can't think about anything else. I'm so close, so nearly there.

And then a hand grabs my boot and yanks my body down.

CHAPTER 20

I shout, my fingers scrabbling for purchase on the rocks as I'm dragged down. My name is called in chorus, but I can't look anywhere but below me. The spy I followed, now cloakless and clad in black, grips my ankle. Her jaw is clenched tight.

I brace myself and kick, but she hangs on, pulling me until I feel like my fingers will break. I can't hold on any more, and a noise comes out of me that I've never made before—a scared whimper. The rocks below are so far away, so sharp and solid that I can almost feel them. I'm falling.

Someone grabs my wrist and heaves upwards. Sasha. Her face is above mine, brow furrowed with effort, teeth clenched.

"Get off my *sister*," she spits out, and she pulls my arm up, securing my hand in a fissure. I kick with renewed effort until I feel the grip on my ankle loosen, and then I wrench my boot up and down, connecting with something soft—an arm, maybe. The spy lets go and I shoot up, clambering over the rocks, yelling at Sasha to come on, hurry up, *move*.

Feliks shouts from above, first my sister's name and then mine. I look up and see his face, twisted with worry, his hair hanging down. He's made it—he's reached the top.

Below me, Inessa's spy has stopped. She's clutching the cliff face with one hand, her other arm held close to her body. Her teeth are bared, though whether in pain or rage I can't tell. I keep going, climbing with shaking legs and numb hands, Sasha by my side, until Feliks grabs a handful of my furs and tugs until I'm up, gasping and rolling over on the snow, lying flat on my back on the cliff top with the cold wind blowing in my face and the white sky spreading wide above me.

When I try to flex my fingers, I can't. So I lie there, panting, until Sasha joins me.

"About time." Someone pulls my mittens from my pockets.

"Katia?"

A pale braid swings in my face, and she puts my mittens on me like my mother did when I was little.

"Don't sound so surprised," she says. "Water I do not like. Heights? Not a problem."

I look across at Sasha on the snow. Her eyes are closed, and she's breathing fast and hard. Beyond her, Anatol's face appears, his dark hair clinging in damp strands to his temples.

Feliks runs to help him up just as Nicolai clears the edge of the cliff. I lift myself on to my elbows, fresh panic quickening my heartbeat.

"They've stopped climbing. There's no one behind us," Anatol gasps out.

Feliks lies on his stomach at the edge and peers down. I scramble around to join him. It's true—the spy is making a slow descent using only one hand. Anastasia's boat bobs out on the sea, almost at her ship. Inessa and the rest of her spies stand at the bottom of the cliff.

And the six of us are on a cliff top in the wind and snow, miles from the city and even farther from the mountain pass, while a fleet of warships heads around the curve of the bay.

Feliks's elbow knocks mine. "What do we do now?"

Anatol's boots scuff the snow next to us. "We head for the mountain pass. If we can find my mother, she'll be queen of Demidova again. She'll imprison Inessa for treason and send ships after the Pyots'kan fleet."

I get to my feet and stand in front of him. He looks so tired, so torn. But I know exactly how it feels to want to give everything to save your family.

"Anatol," says Sasha, "we all understand—we do. But we have to head to the city, to the palace, and raise the alarm."

Nicolai bites his lip, looking at his prince. "We could split up. Three to the city, three to the pass."

I open my mouth, then pause.

"Valor?" Sasha pleads with her eyes. She's thinking about Queen Ana—I know she is—but she's also thinking about what Queen Ana would want us to do now. What Demidova needs us to do.

"We must stay together and go to the city." I hold up my hand as Anatol begins to protest. "Anatol, I want to rescue the queen, believe me. I want to with all my heart. But we won't make it to the pass without horses. And the swiftest horses are in the palace stables."

"We'll be too late," he says.

Maybe he's right. I falter, but Sasha touches my arm. She places her mitten on my sleeve and traces down the thin, silvery scar that runs the length of my forearm. It's been a sign that she'll back me on anything ever since the incident that caused it. Sasha and the princess had been trying to coax a cat down from the top of some heavy drapes, and I'd been summoned to help. The cat had clawed my arm, and I'd dropped it. The cat was fine, but the princess was frantic. I knew right then how much trouble I was in, even as I stood with blood dripping between my fingers and my whole arm on fire.

I didn't hear what the princess shouted at me. I was afraid Sasha wouldn't take my side, but then my sister stepped forward and started talking. After that I was taken to the palace doctor and salved and bandaged. My arm throbbed, and I thought about what had happened all day. It was the first time I was ever afraid Sasha wouldn't take my side.

And until the Magadanskyan palace, it was the last.

But as I stand there with a wicked wind blowing in my face, I hear all the words she just said about me to Anastasia and Inessa, and I know she meant them. The hot ember of hurt smarting in the core of me goes out as though the snow around us has been heaped on it.

I smile at my sister. "We can do both," I say, though Anastasia's words are as fresh as brands in my mind. "But if we don't start now, we'll do neither."

I look out across the desolate lands lying between us and the city. They stretch into the distance, white and unending, studded with farm buildings here and there.

Then we start walking.

The crunch of snow under boots is the only sound until a screech echoes across the land. A lone bird of prey plummets to the ground, and a small brown shape skitters over the snow near the first farm building we reach. The doors and windows are shuttered fast against the cold and wind. The bird lands talons down, its beak piercing its prey and then wrenching back.

I turn to the others and see Sasha's face. Her ankle is still bothering her, and she hasn't said a word.

"Wait here." I break into a run and head for the barn, steering clear of the farmhouse. Maybe I can find a donkey, or even a horse, that we can borrow.

The slatted wooden door creaks. I freeze. A goat bleats, but nothing else happens, so I pull the door open fast. Inside there's a cow, two goats and a pig with six tiny piglets snuffling in straw. The goats look at me and bleat louder, so I make a hasty exit and stop only to shake my head at the others' questions before we carry on.

By the third farm, we've slowed considerably. Sasha still hasn't complained, but we all keep stealing looks at her, and it's plain to see she won't make it.

I squeeze through a gap in a gate to get to the next barn. Chickens squawk their mistrust at me, and I almost leave right away, but then I see him—one cart horse, with great shaggy fetlocks. He cants his head when I step forward, snickering at me.

I tell myself it's not stealing, only borrowing, as I open the stable door and lead him outside. A glance at the farmhouse tells me no one's watching.

"Valor, we can't," says Sasha.

"It's . . . commandeering," I say, though I feel my cheeks flush. "In the name of the queen. For the good of the country."

"The country will thank us more if we take this too," says Feliks, brushing snow from the seat of a cart.

We hitch the cart to the horse behind the cover of the barn, and then, with Prince Anatol's assurances that we'll return both horse and cart along with compensation for their use, everyone piles into the cart, and I urge the huge horse through the snow and onwards to the city.

We pass through farmlands and villages thick with winter, then at last the outskirts of the city. Near the palace we hitch the horse.

"What do we do now?" Feliks asks nervously. He doesn't like being in plain sight so close to the palace. I've been thinking about what to do when we got here the whole way back. Feliks isn't going to like what I have in mind.

"There's no time to be subtle; we have to get to my father." I don't even break stride. "You don't have to come, Feliks. Or you, Katia," I say. "Sasha and I can do it."

Feliks drops back, but a few seconds later he's right next to me. "No way. I'm not missing out on this now, after everything I've done these past couple of weeks."

"Me neither," says Katia.

"We played every hand we had. This is a bigger risk now," says Sasha, keeping pace at my side now that her ankle is rested.

I raise my eyebrow. "Isn't everything we do a big risk?"

The guard at the gates straightens. Recognition flickers across her face, along with a resigned sort of annoyance—she remembers Sasha and me from last time.

"Official business," I say in a loud voice.

"Queen Inessa is not here to receive visitors," says the guard.

"It's just as well that we are not here to see her, then." I tilt my chin up. "We need to speak to the queen's advisers, the general of the Guard, the admiral of the Navy and likely the stablemaster too."

The guard's mouth drops open slightly, but she stands firm. "On whose authority? The queen is not—"

"On mine." Anatol takes a swift step forward and removes the hood of his cloak.

The guard is even more taken aback now. She looks more carefully at all of us, frowning when she meets Feliks's scowling face.

I gamble on her not being privy to Inessa and Anastasia's plans and pray to the saints that she joined the Guard because she cares more about our country than they apparently do.

"Look," I say, "do you think any of us, least of all the prince, in his situation, would turn up here if the fate of the country didn't depend on it? A fleet of Pyots'kan ships launched from a secret bay along the coast, and they'll be passing by our harbour any minute now, so if you have any care for your own personal safety or that of your family, you will escort us immediately to my father. If I'm wrong, you can arrest me yourself."

I take a breath and wait while the guard presses her lips together.

"Come with me," she says.

I exchange glances with Anatol and my sister as we follow the guard through the gates and the garden and into the palace. Feliks's eyes are as round as targets as we hurry through the great hall, up the staircase and down various corridors.

Eventually, we come to a set of double doors. The guard gives us a wary look. "There were . . . orders," she says as she swings them open.

There, at a desk, his hands clutched in his hair as he reads a book lying open before him, is Father. He looks up in surprise, and his face crumples even as his sharp eyes take in the six of us.

The guard clears her throat. "These girls say—"

I cut the guard off, talking as I run with Sasha to Father. He folds both of us into his arms and doesn't ask me to stop or slow down or repeat myself. He just listens, though I feel him gasp quietly several times as I explain.

When I'm finished, and Sasha has added a few bits, I pull away from Father. His face is grave, dark circles under his eyes. But there's no time to ask what happened to him.

I glance at a clock on the marble mantelpiece. "Inessa must be returning soon."

Father steps forward, hesitating when he locks eyes with the guard. They look at each other for a long moment, and then she steps aside. He nods and flies from the room, Sasha and I flanking him, Anatol and Nicolai behind, Katia and Feliks bringing up the rear. I can hear Feliks making little noises of surprise every time we pass a piece of art or walk across a mosaicked floor.

We pass a few servants, and all of them register wide-eyed shock before lowering their gazes to the floor. Father ignores them, a frown etched deep into his features. Eventually we stop at a small door. Father opens it without knocking and disappears inside. I glimpse a desk heaped high with papers and a heavily stocked bookcase before the door swishes shut.

"What's happening?" asks Feliks. Sasha opens her mouth, but before she can speak, the door opens again, and several harried junior advisers rush out and disperse down the hallways. Father stands in the doorway and takes a deep breath.

"My mother—" Anatol begins, but suddenly the sound of footfalls seems to come from everywhere at once.

"I will make sure *everything* that can be done to rescue her will be done," says Father, and then he's off again, winding through the hallways, the rest of us half running to keep up. Advisers flock to Father as soon as we emerge into the main corridor. All around are tight faces, information being exchanged, terse orders being given. I can barely keep up with the sudden commotion.

As we sweep down the central staircase, Father issues commands, and servants fall away to see his bidding done. I hurry to keep pace with him as he calls for other advisers, for reports from the armoury and the garrison. Out of a window, I see riders arriving on foam-covered horses, the news they've been given plainly visible in their frantic haste. The Queen's Guard assembles in the grounds, all heavy boots and shouted orders.

"I'm sorry, but you must wait here. You'll be safe in the palace." Father barely pauses as he sweeps into a chamber containing a long table, the seats already half-filled with members of the immediate court. I recognise many of the faces—women and men who work with my father and mother.

Father stands at the head of the table, and he and Sasha share a bleak look that's cut off by the closing of the doors and the waft of air that accompanies the solid sound of them shutting on us.

We stand in stunned silence for a few seconds.

"What . . . What's happening?" asks Feliks.

"They're going to decide on a course of action, and then . . . do what's best for the country," says my sister.

Anatol kicks the thick carved marble of a table in the hallway. "If I were a girl, I'd be in there making those decisions. They'd be listening to *me*."

Sasha says nothing, but the way she presses her lips together plants a question like a seed inside me.

"Look!" Anatol strides over to a window that faces the square outside. Beyond the gardens and the gates and the square itself is a lone rider, her braids flying, her horse's hooves clattering on the cobbles. I press a hand to the glass beside Anatol. The rider's arms are bare, and I see the black marks twining up them. A Peacekeeper, riding in the streets of Demidova.

Faces press against business windows, and some people run into the streets, bewildered. The guards are all assembled in the palace grounds, and as if that wasn't a strange-enough sight, now comes the surreal spectacle of a Peacekeeper. I bet the six of us standing here are the only ones gazing on this scene who've seen such a thing before.

The Queen's Guard streams out of the gates on foot, and the Peacekeeper has to slow, her horse picking its way through the marching mass. "They're heading to the harbour," says Nicolai.

"All of them?" I peer around the grounds, but in a few short minutes, they've emptied.

Nicolai scans the flood of women and men in the streets. "I think so, yes. Why?"

"Because if they're sending all our forces to the harbour . . ." I whirl to Sasha. "What about the queen?"

Sasha's eyes are wide. She looks exactly the way she did when she pilfered that pastry from the palace kitchen all those years ago.

"Why would a Peacekeeper be here?" I ask. "Why would the whole Guard be sent to the harbour?" I look straight at her. I won't be able to take it if she tries to keep something from me again. "Don't—"

"I won't," she says quickly. "I'll tell you exactly what I think, I promise. I think . . . I think maybe it's not a good tactic to send the Guard anywhere else."

"What about Mother?" demands Anatol.

Sasha's face is pleading, begging us to understand. "If we want to stop a war, we have to send our own fleet after the Pyots'kan ships as fast as possible." She looks to Nicolai, who nods.

"*All* the guards have to go after those ships?" asks Feliks.

Nicolai bites his lip. "It's standard orders," he says. "If there's a threat of this size to the country, then the whole Guard must mobilise. It's what Queen Ana would have ordered if she were here."

"Anatol," Sasha begins.

He throws his hands up in the air. "I must speak to your father at once. I will command him to send half the Guard to the mountain pass." He rushes to the door of the chamber, but I haven't taken my eyes off my sister's face while she's been talking, so I dart there at the same time and stop him, my hand over his on the handle.

"Wait. Let her finish."

Anatol's chest is heaving. He stares at me for a second, and then I feel his grip relax.

"The mountain pass is too small to permit a whole army through undetected," Sasha says. "That's why there's no point in sending part of the Guard up there. But Father would *never* just ignore the plight of Queen Ana. You can rest assured that he'll send the best spies, the very best of the guards to bring her back. It's just that . . ."

"What?" I ask.

She lifts her shoulders. "It will be a very small contingent."

Anatol takes in a breath.

"But that will be for the best," Sasha protests.

"It's also a risk," he says. He takes his hand off the door altogether. "An unacceptable one."

Just then, the doors to the chamber are flung wide, and Father and all the other advisers hurry out, some speaking, some clutching papers, all of them grim and purposeful. Father's gaze lands on us, but then he drags it away, forcing himself to focus on the general of the Guard as she speaks to him.

A lone piece of paper falls from the table in the empty chamber, and Father and the others disappear down the hallway, their footsteps and voices trailing off until we're left standing in silence.

"I want to see for myself who they're sending to the pass," says Anatol. He starts striding in the direction of the stables.

"Wait," I say.

"Valor, she's my *mother*," he says. "What other family do I have left?"

"I know. I *agree* with you. But I know a better way than marching in there like the prince of Demidova."

Anatol presses his lips together for a long moment.

"Do you trust me?" I ask.

His face softens. "Of course I do."

"Then follow me."

I lead the way down some back stairs and corridors used only by palace staff until we come to a window that looks directly over the roof of the stables.

Sasha frowns. "Didn't we . . . ?"

I nod. "Once."

We've done this before—on a dare from a stableboy. He bet that we couldn't climb out on to the roof and swing to the hay bales inside. He was right.

"Is this necessary?" Nicolai looks around anxiously as I swing a leg over the windowsill.

Feliks sniffs and casts a sideways glance at Sasha. "It's *always* better to observe first and then decide on a plan."

Sasha smiles at him, and his neck goes dark red.

"Come on, then," I say, beckoning the others out as I scramble to the edge of the roof and drop to my stomach. They all follow suit until we're lined up and peeking over the gables. The smell of hay and horses and manure filters through on the cold breeze.

Below us, horses snort steam into the air and toss their heads, picking up on the haste with which they're being saddled. Women and men in cloaks shout orders and ready weapons taken from the stocks in the stables. The party being sent to rescue Queen Ana numbers six. I don't know who they are, so I look to Anatol. His brow is furrowed.

We were only just in time—the riders look ready, and in less than a minute, hooves ring out on the cobbles of the paddock and away through the royal family's private grounds. A lone stableboy quiets the remaining horses as the clatter of the departure still sings in the air.

Above us there's a bang and a click, and I look up in time to see a servant moving away through the now-closed window.

Katia's face registers alarm. "How are we going to get back in?"

"We can get down from here," I say, pointing at the hay bales below. "If you hang and swing just right, you can land on those."

Sasha raises her eyebrows. "You came back after we lost that bet and did it without me?"

I hesitate. I never told her I did that. Not after she couldn't do it herself.

She shakes her head. "Never mind. Let's just get down there now." And before I have the chance to say anything else, she's lowering herself off the edge of the roof until she hangs by her hands. She swings back and forth. My heart jumps into my throat, but she tucks her hurt ankle under her and lands on the hay, falling on to her side with a soft noise and a startled cry from the stableboy.

She turns and gestures that she's OK.

I smile. She never would have done that before Tyur'ma.

Sasha says something to the boy while the rest of us drop down, and in short order we're all dusting off our clothes while Anatol dismisses the boy, who clutches his cap and nods enough to make his head fall off.

Anatol waits until the boy has scurried off, and then we look at each other. His gaze wanders to the saddles.

I look at the horses, then back at Anatol.

"You don't have to," he says. "I wouldn't expect it."

"Wait a minute." Katia stops picking hay out of her braids. "You said you wanted to *see*. And now you've seen. Weren't those six riders the best the Guard has to offer?"

Nicolai nods. "They were. The queen couldn't have picked better herself."

"That may be true," says Anatol. "But still . . ."

"I'm going with you," I say flatly.

He looks torn.

"I have to go," he says. "My mother needs me. My *country* needs me."

"As does mine," I say. "I don't intend to have gone through these past weeks for nothing. You won't get there without my help, anyway. You may remember I have some skill with a crossbow."

I see the hint of a smile on his face before he moves to grab a saddle.

Sasha straightens up from rubbing her sore ankle, and I take her hands.

"I know," she says, resignation in her voice. "Of course you're going. But remember that Father will send the best archers. Their small numbers mean they can approach with stealth. You need to do the same."

"Not *all* the best archers," Anatol calls over. "I have one of them with me."

"I'm coming too," says Nicolai.

"No," I say. "You should catch up with the rest of the Guard. We need to know what Anastasia's doing. You can be our eyes and ears at the docks."

Nicolai frowns as though confused. "I don't remember you becoming general or queen recently, Valor."

"What do you m—? Oh. I'm not giving orders, Nicolai, I'm just *suggesting* that—"

"Listen to Valor's *suggestion*, please, Nicolai," says Anatol.

"Of course, Prince Anatol." He gives an exaggeratedly formal bow.

"That's settled, then," says Sasha, wiping a smile off her face. "I'll return to the palace and find Father. My skills will be put to best use with him. I'll try to persuade him to send reinforcements to the pass."

"Stay safe." I pull her into a tight hug.

"She'll be safe with us. I'll stay with her to protect her," says Feliks fiercely.

Katia puts her hand on his shoulder. "What Feliks means is—"

"Inessa has returned!" Sasha breaks in. Her gaze is locked on the palace windows. On the inside, servants and Inessa's guards hurry past.

Sasha turns to us. "Go! Before she stops you."

"What about you?" I ask.

"We'll deal with her," says Katia, setting her mouth in a stubborn line. "Let's go."

The three of them hurry away. I glance back at Sasha as I mount a grey mare, who's skittish underneath me as I gather the reins. Sword at his side, Anatol rides out of the paddock to rescue the queen, and I follow him.

CHAPTER 21

The ground is hard beneath the snow, and the steam of the horses' breath punctuates the air as they find their stride, eager to burn off nervous energy.

We take a circuitous route around the dense inner city and out to the valley—an hour's hard ride at best. The cold is harsh, pinching my face and seeping through my furs. Every nerve in my body is on fire, though, as I urge my horse onwards. Prince Anatol rides as well as I do, and the palace horses are fine and strong.

I quickly work out that Anatol intends to take the more difficult trail across the top of the land, leaving the party of six to ride low in the valley along the same route Peacekeeper Rurik took when Feliks and I travelled to Tyur'ma. The bare branches of trees whip into my path, and though the horses are forced to slow their headlong pace, it still takes every ounce of concentration I have to stay seated and keep my wits about me.

Time seems to pass differently, and though I register that I'm getting both hungry and thirsty, it's just a dim and detached feeling—one that I push aside. It starts to snow, and I think about Queen Ana, and about Anastasia on her ship, determined to forge an alliance with Pyots'k no matter the cost. I think about Mother too, and wonder where she is, whether she's safe. Ahead of me, Anatol pulls up short as the valley flattens out and the forest becomes sparse. Movement to our left catches my eye. I grip the saddle between my thighs, pull my crossbow from my back and nock a bolt. Anatol touches my arm. "Just a stag," he says. I realise that I've pulled my horse up in front of his, shielding him. His face is pink from the pace of our journey and exposure to the freezing air, errant flakes of snow melting slowly in his hair and on his cloak.

I look back. The stag's antlers are visible now at the treeline, but it doesn't venture out on to the plain. I lower my bow.

"Sorry," I whisper.

He shakes his head. "I'm glad you're here."

My horse tosses its mane and steps forward. "Ride," I tell the prince. His horse fidgets under him at the nervous edge in my voice. "Ride fast."

I grasp the reins in my cold hands, and we surge forward on to the plain. Snow packs down under the horses' hooves, but they're used to it. They'll tire quickly after all they've already done, but we can't afford to spare them now.

My legs ache, unused to riding for so long at such a pace, but I don't slow my horse. The flurries blind us, but flashes of the stone walls of Tyur'ma up ahead show through when the wind whips the falling snow away.

I keep us heading straight for the shadow of the mountain, locking my eyes again and again on Tyur'ma. I'm riding towards it voluntarily, a free girl, but it still freezes my heart. I know how it feels to take the prison cart through the portcullis.

My throat burns with the cold. The wisps of hair that have escaped my *ushanka* soon gather a crust of ice. The snow falls thicker. I can't tell which direction is which any more.

"Valor!"

The prince has drawn his sword. I see nothing—just the snow bearing down on us—but an arrow sticks out of his mount, just above the shoulder. The horse twists back and forth, and Anatol clings to it.

"Anatol!"

I whip my head around, my breath harsh and loud, and draw my crossbow. But I can't see anything. Or anybody.

The prince's horse rears so high that he drops back, falling into the snow with a soft thud. His horse bolts, using the last of its energy to buck as it disappears into the blinding whiteness that surrounds us.

"Anatol." I blink snow from my lashes, desperate to unleash my bolt if only I could see where I should aim. But my horse is snorting and tossing its head, nervous and exhausted, and I can't manage both horse and bow. The prince hauls himself up from the snow.

"Are you all right?" I ask. "Where did that arrow come from?" It takes me by surprise just how much it scared me to think he might be hurt.

He shakes his head, breathing hard.

I squint up at the battlements of Tyur'ma, but it's no use—I can't see anything.

I offer Anatol my hand. "We have to keep moving. Get on."

We both know the horse won't get far with two of us riding, but right now I can't think beyond getting us close, and in one piece, to the mountain.

Anatol mounts my horse, sitting behind me, and we're off again, struggling through the snow. My hands are frozen on the reins, my toes numb in my boots.

I start at every noise, and the only comfort I have is the thought that whoever's out there, whoever loosed that arrow, can see no better than we can.

The mountain looms, and it's only the well-lit walls of Tyur'ma that give me any indication of where we are and how close we've got to the pass. I hope Sasha and the others are safe back at the palace. The thought makes me spur the horse on harder, though the poor creature doesn't have much more to give.

Minutes later, Anatol leans forward. "Valor? We'll have to walk the rest."

He's right. The horse is struggling, its head dipping lower with every stride. Ahead of us, the snow begins to rise as we reach the outcroppings of the mountain. We must climb to the pass.

Anatol swings down from the saddle, and I lurch forward and drop, stumbling into the snow. I steady myself, and we leave the horse. There's nothing to hitch it to, and we can't force it to stay.

"Can you see . . . anything?" Anatols asks.

I shake my head, tired and sodden, but every nerve on edge. I point to the pass, and Anatol nods. We both turn and scrabble up, up, up the snow-covered rocks. My hands and feet are clumsy with cold, but my heart races.

Anatol points to a steep outcropping of rock, and I nod my understanding. He wants to overlook the pass. I drag myself the last few yards, my hands hardly able to grip any more, and pull myself up next to Anatol. He's crouched behind some boulders. The white stone is veined through with minerals, like the cliff-face entrance to the mines in Tyur'ma. I scoop out the snow to make a shelter and conceal us better. My fingers sting and ache from the ride. They won't bend properly, so I use my forearms. Anatol helps, and then we sit, panting, for a few seconds before we turn and peek out over the scene below.

The pass is narrow, razor-sharp rock deceptively covered with a soft coating of powdery snow.

Anatol sucks in a breath. A small group of Inessa's guards surrounds a shaking woman. They wear heavy furs, while her thin cloak ripples in the wind. On her head, a *kokoshnik* sits askew.

"Queen Ana," I say, at the same time Anatol cries "Mother!"

How long have they been standing there?

Anatol's hand moves to his sword, and he plants one foot in the snow.

"Wait," I say. Out on the plain beyond the pass, on Pyots'kan soil, I see movement in the snow—something strange. I would think it a flock of tiny dark birds, but the movement is all wrong. I pull Anatol back down beside me.

"What is that?" he asks.

I narrow my eyes against the snowfall and see the glint of cold winter light on steel.

"People," I whisper. Women and men dressed all in white, their furs virtually undetectable against the snow on the plain. The dark marks I can see are their weapons. Hundreds upon hundreds of them, armed with swords and bows, march across the plain towards the unforgiving white mountain and the black walls of Tyur'ma.

Anatol sees it too. "Soldiers." His voice is hushed. "The Pyots'kan army."

CHAPTER 22

Snow deadens all sound, so it seems as though a ghost army marches towards us in a dream world of muted light and slowly falling snowflakes.

Anatol and I look at each other. All the colour has blanched from his face.

"Where's the rescue party?" he whispers.

They should have been ahead of us, taking the easier route through the valley. Are they still approaching the pass? Hidden in the trees somewhere?

The prince looks over his shoulder, searching the forest. It's silent and empty. His breath mists the air. Once. Twice.

Then one of Inessa's guards moves, and I catch a glimpse of a cloak. It's a figure, on his knees in the snow, hands bound behind his back. It's one of the rescue party.

My heart sinks. I nudge Anatol.

When he sees too, he clenches his jaw. "Are they all there?"

"I don't know. But . . ."

He lets out a measured breath. If one is captured, and they all rode together, it's likely they've all been captured.

I wish that were the worst thing about the scene I see before me. My thoughts fracture like thin ice on a lake. The mountain pass is too small to permit a whole army to march through undetected, but—

"This must be why that Peacekeeper was going to the palace," I say. "They saw this from the walls of Tyur'ma and sent a warning."

Anastasia never mentioned this; in all her gloating she only said the queen was to be handed over to Pyots'k at the pass. Did she want us to see this? Did she even know about it?

"The Peacekeeper will have raised the alarm." Anatol's voice is faint. "The Guard will have turned away from the docks by now. They'll be headed here. There'll be a battle."

I don't answer him. I already know. There's going to be a war. Right here in Demidova. And not in months or years to come because of Anastasia's allowing Pyots'k to launch its ships—but right now, because their army is invading.

"We have to close the pass." I blurt out the words fast before I even begin to think of how impossible it is. "It's the only way to prevent a war."

Anatol's expression moves from animated to hopeless as he realises the same thing I do—the only way to stop this is to do something that can't be done.

"Valor," he says gently, "it's a wonderful idea. But we'd need something more than a boy with a sword and a girl with a crossbow to do that." He casts his eyes over the steep sides of the pass, but his expression doesn't change. He shakes his head. "We'd need something powerful enough to cause a landslide."

He's right. But there must be a way. There must.

I follow his gaze. The snow has fallen in such a thick layer over the pass that the smaller trees are bent almost in half with the weight of it on their branches.

I grab his arm. "Not a landslide," I say. "An *avalanche*."

He frowns, and then his eyebrows shoot up.

The first of the soldiers in white is almost at the pass now. Very soon he'll be into Demidova, and they won't stop until the whole army has poured through while everyone in the city is distracted by Anastasia's ships sailing past our harbour.

"How?" he says. "And what about Mother?"

"We have to get her out of there first. That's your job." I say. "Then I can shoot into the snow and break it up. Look how steep the sides of the pass are. After that flurry we just had, it will fall, I know it."

I don't know it, but I can't sit here and do nothing.

"It has to be now," I say. "Before the Pyots'kan army gets through the pass."

Antol's jaw tenses. He nods.

We creep around the boulders and out into the open. Below, the soldiers approaching the pass march on despite the dangerous glint of the rock through the snow.

I crouch low, and Anatol follows suit, but we're both wearing dark furs, and I'm painfully aware of how visible we are. The guards surrounding Queen Ana all have their eyes trained on the approaching Pyots'kan force, though, and as we get closer, I let myself wonder if we might be able to pull this off.

I'm barely breathing by the time we're near enough to see that all six members of the rescue party kneel in the snow beyond Inessa's guards. Their hands are bound behind them. I move my head a fraction to the left and catch Anatol's eye.

A shout rings across the snow, and my head snaps back.

The guards have seen us.

I whip my crossbow from my back. "Get behind me," I say. And before I can give it a second thought, I'm running, slipping and sliding downhill, new snow rushing with me, Anatol's harsh breaths behind. One of the rescuers launches to her feet and barrels into two of the guards, one of whom was already releasing an arrow. It whistles through the air and my heart stops, but it falls short.

More arrows fly past as we skitter over ice and rocks that I don't feel any more, though I know how sharp they are.

I dig my heels into fresh snowfall to slow my descent. Anatol skids to a halt next to me. I hold up my crossbow and take aim at a guard. Then everything speeds up—the other rescuers follow the lead of the first woman and leap to their feet to attack Inessa's guards. Queen Ana draws one of the guard's swords with a ring of metal that echoes around the pass and wields it while backing away. Anatol rushes forward to his mother, drawing his own sword and taking up a stance next to her.

I circle around the guard my bolt is pointing at until I'm next to Anatol.

"Cut their bonds, Anatol," says the queen. He turns swiftly and releases the rescue party.

Inessa's guards look to the one who must be their leader. She's tight-lipped, her eyes flashing, but she shakes her head, and Queen Ana's rescue party surges forward and disarms the guards who still hold weapons.

The first of the Pyots'kan soldiers enters the pass. There's no time to explain.

"Run!" I say to Anatol.

Queen Ana holds her sword aloft, and we scramble backwards, up towards the overhang where Anatol and I hid before. The rescue party falls into place around the queen, and Anatol and I stand in front. My legs ache and my crossbow keeps dipping as my boots sink into the snow and throw me off balance.

"What are you doing here?" I hear Queen Ana say. "Where is your sister? And the Guard? What of Demidova? Those ships . . ." Her breath is coming in gasps, but even though she's frozen to her bones and her country is under imminent threat of attack, her voice is commanding.

"We must get above the pass, back on to the mountain," says Anatol, just as out of breath. "Valor has a plan."

I stumble back as we reach the top of the incline and the ground levels out. From this vantage point, we can see for miles in either direction, but as the front ranks of the soldiers in white enter the pass from Pyots'kan soil, snow starts to fall again, slowly for a few seconds and then thick and fast. Unarmed now, Inessa's guards run towards the Pyots'kan end of the pass.

On the Demidovan side, out on the plain, black furs and gold sashes stand starkly against the snow, and the muted sounds of called orders and snorting horses filter through. It's a unit of the Queen's Guard. The snow-blind battle is about to come to us—if I don't stop it first.

"Valor!" Anatol pushes forward, outside the protective circle of the rescue party. We're both breathing hard.

I raise my crossbow and aim at an overhang of snow, blinking away fat flakes, and let a bolt fly. It embeds in the snow. I squint, hoping so hard to see movement that I clench my fists around my bow.

"Help her!" It's the queen, ordering the rescue party. Four of the six have bows, either their own or taken from Inessa's guards, and they step forward instantly and aim as I did. I nock another bolt and join them, and we shoot in unison.

Nothing happens for a beat, but then there's a slight slide that I see only because the dark dots of the bolts move.

"Again!" I cry.

The two guards next to me look at each other first, but they do as I say. We reload and release again. I stare intently, willing it to work, all my thoughts bent on it. The snowy overhang creaks and cracks and then starts to slide. It builds up speed, and Inessa's guards shout as the snow falls like rolling waves into the pass.

My mouth has dried out, the anticipation tensing every muscle in my body.

"The other side!" I shout over the noise. A wolf's howl echoes around the mountain, and a horse's panicked cry answers it. There are shouts from the pass as Inessa's guards and Pyots'kan soldiers flee from the falling snow.

We shoot and shoot again, but there's no overhang on the right side, and the snow won't fall.

A wall of snow still tumbles from the left, crashing down into the pass. The Pyots'kan army retreats, taking Inessa's guards with them, but there's a mass of soldiers building at the entrance to the pass. Waiting. All I've done is delay them.

"It's not enough," I say, swinging wildly to Anatol.

Queen Ana joins us. "The Guard is almost here," she says. Halfway across the plain, I can see a swarm of black and gold showing through the snowfall. She puts her hand on my shoulder. "There's nothing we can do to stop the battle now."

I shake my head. "If we close the pass, they can't get through. *Ever.*"

The queen presses her lips together, kind but firm. She nods to the slowing tumble of snow in the pass. "You've bought the Guard enough time to get here. Trust in them. With any luck, we'll keep the battle out here on the plains, far from the city."

It's not enough. My whole family is back there. All my friends. All the people of Demidova.

"Your Highness?" One of the rescuers offers the queen a thick cloak and starts talking about battle strategy, pointing out spots to place archers.

I catch Anatol's eye and take a step back, then another and another. He frowns but follows me until we're both behind the rescue party.

"We need to close the pass for good," I say.

He shrugs a little impatiently. "I agree. *Everyone* agrees with you, Valor. But the fact remains that we can't." He spreads his empty hands.

"What if we could, though?"

"Then we should do it, of course. But—"

"Come on."

I dash back down the path and then veer sharply to the right. The black walls of Tyur'ma rise ahead of us. The torches on top of the wall, already lit, blink tiny firelights into the white sky. I keep running straight towards the prison, feeling almost as though I'm fighting my way through the falling snow as well as what's already on the ground. After a few minutes, I scramble up the path to the portcullis— the same path Peacekeeper Rurik's cart struggled up months ago when Feliks and I arrived here.

"What are you *doing*?" Anatol gasps, but he doesn't slow down.

I reach the gridded iron of the narrow door and look up, up, up to the top of the wall. A shudder passes through me, and it's not from the cold of the iron under my hands.

I shake the door, my fingers gripping the bars, yelling at the top of my voice. "I know you're watching me. In the name of the queen, open the door!"

I stand back and wait, the cold air searing my throat. Anatol stares at me as though I've lost my mind.

Behind us, the Queen's Guard is close. If the ground were free of snow, I'd probably be able to hear their boots marching by now.

I open my mouth to scream again, but the portcullis rattles and starts to open. I don't wait for it to rise fully, ducking under it as soon as I can. Anatol bites his lip but follows. The passageway between the two walls is empty, so I bolt along it and around a corner.

The cage I entered with Feliks and Peacekeeper Rurik is there, just as I remember. I don't think I'll ever forget it. I slow at the sight, but then force myself to speed up again until we're standing in front of the grid of bars.

There, on the other side, her grey furs as immaculate as ever and her eyes just as cold, stands Warden Kirov.

CHAPTER 23

"To what do we owe this pleasure?" The warden's voice is still like a bucket of ice water to the face, but I don't let myself shiver. I know she knows what's happening beyond her walls.

"I need to close the pass. You have to give us the blasting powder used in the mines." I dig my elbow into Anatol's side.

"By order of Queen Ana of Demidova, who has just been . . . liberated," he says. I hope Warden Kirov doesn't hear the lie in his voice like I do.

Her gaze flicks to him, but comes back to me.

I tilt my chin up. "We've rescued the rightful queen from Inessa's guards. The queen regent is working with Anastasia and Pyots'k, and I know you've seen the approaching soldiers. We are about to be overrun by the Pyots'kan army.

This isn't about settling any score between me and you, it's about—"

Warden Kirov steps forward, and I break off as she unlocks the cage between us. She doesn't take her eyes off me while she does it. "There's no score between us," she says smoothly, in exactly the tone of voice that lets me know that there is indeed an enormous score between us, and it is most certainly not settled. "Now hurry. There's no time to waste."

For the second time, I step through the cage into the empty grounds of Tyur'ma. The place is silent—locked down, the remaining prisoners confined in their cells. My chest tightens. Warden Kirov calls out orders, and two Peacekeepers I hadn't even seen materialise. One of them is the woman with the eagle tattoo on her back who walked across the grounds the night I escaped from my cell and went to the tower.

The warden speaks low and fast to the Peacekeepers. They run to the mines. I watch them track across the tall drifts of untouched snow in the desolate grounds, my gaze stopping on the empty space where the ice domes stood. I glance across at the infirmary, but it's shuttered like every other building. Nothing moves except our breath on the air. It's preternaturally quiet with the fall of the snow.

At the top of the wall stands a Peacekeeper, a bow in her hands. She stands stock-still and stares at me. I exchange a look with Anatol, one that says we both now know who hit his horse. Did Warden Kirov order it? With the snow as bad as it is, it would have been a difficult shot. Was it meant for the prince, or for me?

I breathe faster, my palms prickling with sweat. I know the Warden can't keep me here this time, but I can't stop the fear that spreads through me like a bloodstain on snow.

But before I know it, the Peacekeepers return and press black tubes capped at both ends—like strange candles with long wicks—into our hands. A Peacekeeper tells me how to set them off, holding fire inch-sticks out for me to take.

Warden Kirov unlocks the cage and I step through, eager to get away. Anatol and a Peacekeeper follow. The Peacekeeper unlocks the other side of the cage, and then we're out in the passageway and I can almost—*almost*—breathe again.

"Valor?"

I hesitate for just a moment, and then turn back to face the warden.

She smiles, as fathomless as ice. "Don't forget to run."

I stare at her while a shiver works its way down my back. Anatol tugs me after the Peacekeeper, and I slide the blasting powder sticks into my pockets as I run. The fire inch-sticks I keep tucked into my mitten, held safe against my palm.

The portcullis rattles upwards by means unseen as we near. Anatol and I dash out under it and down the path.

I take one last look at Tyur'ma. The Peacekeeper stands, his stance wide and his arms crossed, in the narrow doorway, tattooed wolves fighting over his skin as the portcullis slams back into the ground.

"What now?" Anatol's cheeks are flushed, and his eyes are bright but hectic, darting around as we run.

"Take this side of the pass," I say between breaths. "I'll go to the other. We run to the Pyots'kan end and lay charges there first."

The prince nods, no energy or breath left to speak, and I leave him, dropping down the mountain in great leaps, not heeding the Queen's Guard, which is almost at the mouth of the pass now. I race up the rocks to reach the other side of the pass and run down the length of it, glancing across to see Anatol running parallel on his side.

But down in the pass, the soldiers in white are already there, already marching through. I lose my footing and stumble forward, my hands hitting snow and stone, pain jarring up my wrists.

I push upright, running again before I'm even fully standing. My hands sting, and after a few dozen steps, the inside of one of my mittens feels damp. I reach the end of the pass and pull up short. Out on the plain in Pyots'k, the army masses in the shadow of the mountain.

I drop to the ground, my heart beating out of my chest. Anatol stops directly opposite me across the pass. I pull my mittens off my shaking hands, and blood smears up my left palm. I wipe it off on the snow, ignoring the burn, and fish a blasting powder stick out of my pocket. I jam it as deep into the snow as I can and try to wedge it into the rock itself, and then I fumble the fire inch-sticks out of my mitten. There's a red stain on the packet, but the sticks are dry.

The first one blows out instantly, but I strike the second on the exposed rock and cover it so closely that I burn my hand. The long wick fizzes into life, and I take Warden Kirov's advice—I run. Halfway back, I see Anatol. He's been stopped, accosted by half of the rescue party. He's gesturing wildly.

As I drop to set my second charge, the air splits with a *crack*. Instinctively I cover my head. When I turn to see, the pass is clouded with snow and particles of rock. Debris tumbles down the sides. Anatol's first charge has gone off.

I rush to light my second powder stick, jamming it deep into a crevice so that only the fuse shows. Then I run, lurching forward as my first charge goes off. The ground rumbles beneath my feet, and I hear rock crumbling. Shards of stone and snow rain down around me. I desperately want to turn to look, but I don't dare. An arrow flies past me, shot from down in the pass, and then a bolt, so close I feel it on my furs. I dodge away from the edge as much as I can and keep running.

I snatch glimpses of what's happening on the other side of the pass, the queen being hurried away down the mountain, Anatol following her while one member of the rescue party crouches at the beginning of the pass on the Demidovan side. She's lighting another charge.

As she takes off running down the mountainside, I throw myself to the ground and light the last of my own charges, then I follow, skidding, running, half falling and tumbling on the rocks. Ahead of me, the Pyots'kan soldiers who have already made it through the pass spill out on to the plain in Demidova.

The wind whips the snow briefly to one side, the flakes bending like a flock of tiny, delicate birds, and suddenly I see the whole scene. The Pyots'kan soldiers stream through the pass, and just a little way down the mountain, approaching fast, is the Guard.

The two charges above go off within a second of each other with ear-splitting cracks that vibrate my head. Shouts of "Retreat!" ring out and are drowned by a rumbling of rock that feels like it comes from right beneath my feet. I skid to a halt. The sides of the pass shift and slide, gathering momentum; rock and snow, ice and stone cloud the air like foam on waves.

Hope spreads into my frozen heart even as debris starts to spill out of the mouth of the pass and towards me on the slope of the mountain. I run again, down towards the plain, because there's nowhere else to go now.

The first ranks of the Guard clash with the Pyots'kan soldiers who made it through the pass. Shouts underlie the ringing of sword on sword and the whistle of arrows through the air. I spin around, searching for Anatol. A sudden skirmish looms up out of the snow in front of me. I grasp my crossbow and pull it from my back, holding it in front of me in terror.

The soldiers don't notice me, and it's not until the fight has passed away from me as quickly as it came that I realise I never loaded a bolt. I wasn't even armed.

Through the blinding snow I see a flash of dark hair and a familiar face. I open my mouth to call Anatol's name, but then his face changes, contorting in fear. A soldier advances on him. I run, loading my bow as I move, lifting my boots high, shouting out Anatol's name. I throw myself in front of him, crossbow raised, finger hovering over the trigger, ready to release.

"Get away from my friend," I say, though it's more to keep me steady than in hopes that the soldier will hear me. I don't hesitate when it comes to the hunt. But this is not a hunt. The man in front of me is not an animal, he's an adult with a drawn sword, and this feels very real in a way that holding a crossbow has never felt before.

"Valor!" Queen Ana's voice, pitched higher than the shouts on the battlefield, almost draws my attention. She runs straight towards the soldier, swinging her sword back and then forward. The soldier in white drops to the ground, and I wonder, if I'd had to do it myself, could I have?

The queen calls my name again. I see dismay on her face, but I don't understand. Then I look down and see the red stain seeping across my furs. An arrow sticks out of my chest at an angle.

CHAPTER 24

I watch as if in a dream as the Guard fights on around me, as the queen runs forward and as Anatol's hand reaches for me as I drop.

The sky grows dark around the edges, and the pass moves, the mountain moves. Everything tilts, and the ground moves up to meet me.

"You closed the pass, Valor. You did it." Anatol's breath escapes in the smallest cloud, once, and the world goes black.

Bare tree branches interlace in front of a grey sky, and a horse moves under me. My skin is hot, but I'm cold—I must be, because I'm shaking and I can't make it stop. Hands touch me, and faces blur in and out of my vision; it's cold and black again. I wake up and Sasha is there, but my head is too heavy to hold up and my eyes won't focus. Maybe it's a dream.

There's noise behind a door, but the door stays closed, and I can't reach to open it. When I try, my shoulder screams.

I open my eyes. There's a weight on my chest. No—my body is bandaged tightly. I'm in a deep, soft bed, light slanting in through half-drawn red velvet drapes that fall from ceiling to floor. I'm in the palace.

I turn my head. Sasha leaps up from the chair next to the bed, her face alert and pointed, her dark eyes huge. "You're awake. Are you awake? Does it hurt very much?"

"Only when I breathe," I say, and her face relaxes into a smile, though there are tears in her eyes.

I try to take a deep breath, but I can't. "Anatol?" I whisper.

Sasha takes my hand and squeezes my fingers. "He's fine. Though—"

"Though he would like to speak to you himself," comes a voice from beyond the door. "Can I come in?"

"Yes," I say.

Sasha has to repeat it for me. My own voice won't come out loud enough.

Anatol pokes his head around the door, and then steps inside. There are cuts and scrapes on his hands and face, but his clothes are fine and spotless again, and his hair has been forced flat. It's a stark contrast to the last time I saw him.

I try to pull myself up on the pillows and wince. Then my brain catches up with what happened today. Or was it yesterday?

I catch Sasha's other hand with my free one. "Father? *Mother?*" I look to Anatol. "And what of Queen Ana? Did the pass really close? Did the battle end? The ships . . . I . . . Where *is* everyone?"

Sasha and Anatol exchange an amused glance, but there's something else there too.

"What is it?" I ask, pushing up and then falling back again as pain stabs through my shoulder.

"Valor!" Sasha fusses over my pillows, frowning down at me. "We'll answer you, but you have to promise to lie still."

She stares at me sternly until I nod, and then she perches on the side of the bed.

"Father is fine, if busy, working with Queen Ana. He's been at your side as often as he could while you slept, but right now there's so much to do. They made an announcement about her being restored to the throne earlier this morning. Since then they've been hidden away in the queen's chambers, talking over matters of state. The first thing the queen did was send word that Mother must be found and should return to the palace immediately."

Anatol breaks in, flicking his fine cloak over his shoulder as he steps forward. "The battle was over the very minute you got shot," he says. "My mother was furious, and the Guard was instantly galvanised. Any stragglers were rounded up, and now they're all in the cells awaiting sentences. Mother dismissed all of Inessa's guards, and they've fled. Inessa herself—" He leans forward, making sure he has my attention. He does.

"She's in the dungeon right now. Under twenty-four-hour guard. You closed the pass, but Mother stationed half the Guard at Tyur'ma anyway, just in case. My mother and your father are making plans to destroy the tunnel from Pyots'k so none of this can ever happen again. No one ever dreamed Queen Lidiya would use it without permission. But maybe she wouldn't have without Anastasia emboldening her. You saved the country from war, and . . ." He looks at the curtains and then the carpet, then rubs his hand over his hair. "You saved my life. Thank you."

I smile. His hair is sticking up. "Well, I could hardly let anyone else aim a weapon at Prince Anatol of Demidova, could I?"

He grins back. "Of course not. That's your job." His grin fades. I know the look on his face. I've seen it too often since not only his sister but now also his father betrayed their family.

"Where is . . . How is your father?" I ask quietly.

Anatol's face twists, and I wish I hadn't asked. Sasha answers quickly for him. "The King is resting in his chambers in the palace. He is not well, but he realises that his actions were not in the best interests of the country. He will not be appearing during public engagements for the foreseeable future."

I have the feeling that the rest of the country will be hearing a very similar, if not quite identical, speech from Queen Ana very soon. Sasha gives me a look, then glances at Anatol and back to me. I nod. We can talk more about it later.

"What about Anastasia?" I ask.

There's a pause. This is what they didn't want to tell me.

"The ships sailed," says Sasha. "There was no one to stop them in the end—the timing was executed to split the Guard and confuse everyone. Anastasia planned for the Pyots'kan army to distract the Guard and for Inessa to hold her position as queen until Anastasia returned from Saylas. She meant to assume the throne of Demidova, help Queen Lidiya conquer Saylas and then move on Magadanskya with Queen Lidiya's assistance. I can't believe her nerve." Sasha squeezes my hand again.

Anatol nods at my sister. "She would have got away with it if Sasha hadn't persuaded your father to send some of the Guard to the pass, and you hadn't thought of blowing the whole thing up."

"But she got away," I say.

Sasha makes an impatient noise. "Valor, when are you going to realise that you can't do everything yourself? You almost *died*. And you still averted what could have been a huge, bloody battle and reduced it to a few dozen soldiers, all of whom have been captured by the Guard. Isn't that enough for you? Because, let me tell you, it's enough for everyone else."

I open my mouth and then close it. I'm glad about that, glad beyond words. But . . . Anastasia got away.

Sasha and Anatol look at each other again. Something isn't quite right, I can tell. But my head is getting heavy again, and my eyes won't stay open. I fight through the descending fog.

"Where are the others?" I ask, a sudden spike of worry dragging me back up from sleep.

"They're right here in the palace, and they're fine," says Sasha. "Get some more rest, Valor. We'll bring them to see you later, I promise."

I try to nod, reassured, but at the same time I think about Anastasia sailing away on that ship. I should stop. I've been shot, and I need to rest, like Sasha said. I keep telling myself that until I slip away again.

"Are you sure you're ready for this?" Sasha frowns concernedly at me from the mirror. We're both standing in front of the floor-length gilt frame in the dressing room of my sickroom in the palace. Music floats in through the open window. Outside the palace, the festival of Saint Sergius has resumed—the queen decreed it even though the date has passed. "You've done nothing but sleep for two days."

"Which is why I should be there," I say, letting her help me ease a tunic over my head.

"But this whole banquet is in your honour." Sasha tugs and smooths the material into place. "Queen Ana said we could delay until you're ready."

"I'm ready now," I say. "I've had enough of lying in bed."

She tilts her head and raises her eyebrows. "People do tend to do so when they get shot with arrows, or so I hear. I doubt anyone thought you were shirking your duties."

I shake my head. "Queen Ana has resumed all *her* duties. It's time I did too. Mother needs me. And as soon as I get this over with—" I bite my lip and watch my eyes widen in the mirror as Sasha gives me a look.

"Oh, that's not what I meant. I'm very honoured that the queen would . . . What I mean to say is . . ."

Sasha laughs. "I know. I want to get back to my apprenticeship too. But even after today is 'over with', you can hardly ride a horse or hold a bow. Not yet."

I shift my head impatiently as she braids my hair.

There's a knock at the door.

"Come in," I call. It only pulls at my chest a little to raise my voice.

"It's us. Me and Feliks," says Katia from the other room. "Keep still," she says in a lower voice. "How have you got a mark on this tunic already?"

I grin at my sister as she finishes my hair, and we both walk back to the other room. Katia looks taller than ever, though maybe it's because she's holding herself so stiffly in her new clothes. The deep red tunic suits her pale skin. She smiles, looking nervous and excited then nervous all over again.

"How are you, Valor? You look well."

I haven't really spoken to either of them for days. I think they've been in my room, but I've been so tired, and the doctor kept making me drink something that made me lose focus and sleep.

Feliks bounces on his toes, still drinking in every detail of the palace. I don't think he'll ever get used to it.

"I'm fine," I say. "And I'm ready. Let's go." I raise my eyebrows at Sasha. "Where's Nicolai? Didn't you say he was here too?"

"He's been caught up with business at the docks since you went after Queen Ana, but I know he'll be back as soon as he can." She puts her hand on my back and ushers all of us out of the room. "Don't worry about him, Valor—he can take care of himself."

I can hear the strains of music coming from downstairs even before we reach the grand staircase that leads down from the mezzanine to the great hall. My stomach rumbles loudly—I can smell roast chicken and butter and ginger and all manner of other food mingled together.

Someone taps a silver spoon against a crystal glass as I step on to the first stair. It's Lady Olegevna, her glass raised high in front of her. Surrounding dignitaries follow suit, and soon the whole company is greeting us as I walk down the stairs, flanked by Sasha and Feliks on one side and Katia on the other.

At the bottom of the stairs, my parents are waiting. I lock eyes with my mother. This is the first time I've seen her since she was sent away—judging from her riding gear, she's only just arrived. Her expression is one of pride mingled with the kind of infuriation that tells me I may be hearing her opinion of my actions very soon and at great length.

I almost run to her, and to Father, who looks tired and worried but holds tight to Mother's hand. But I've been told I need to stand in position at the bottom of the stairs.

Queen Ana steps forward, Anatol by her side. Her gown sweeps the floor. I smile as Anatol, under pretext of adjusting his cloak, runs a finger under the high, stiff collar of the same gold-embroidered peacock-blue tunic he wore the day

I took aim at him with my crossbow and hit an ice sculpture instead.

"You are ready, Valor?" asks the queen.

I nod.

Two of the Queen's Guard, their gold sashes a welcome sight, open the wide arched doors of the palace, and a buzz of excited noise washes in from the crowd outside. The queen leads the way out into the palace gardens. Beyond the golden gates, trestle tables have been set up in the square, line upon long line. Each of them is laden with food, and the benches on either side are crammed with people.

At the sight of the queen, they all stand. Katia grips my hand as we walk the length of the garden, out through the gates and towards the stone fountain with its great jets of water. As we step up on to the rim behind Lady Olegevna, I see Feliks sticking to Sasha's side, his fingers pinching her sleeve hard enough to bleach the colour out of them.

The queen starts her speech, thanking Lady Olegevna for Magadanskya's continued support, assuring everyone present that the pass between Demidova and Pyots'k is now impassable but still heavily guarded. There's talk about the possibility of a threat from Saylas once Anastasia and the Pyots'kan forces reach their shores, but the queen brings her words back around to the pass and how it was closed. She doesn't speak of what she tasked me with in our meeting under the fountain, doesn't tell everyone even a tenth of what has happened. I hear my father's hand in the words she uses and the ways in which she strings them into ideas.

I listen, but it's hard to concentrate on anything when wafts of hot gravy and soft bread keep spilling from the banquet hall. But when the queen starts talking about Feliks and Katia, I wrench my attention back. This is the part I want to hear.

"Katia Feodora and Feliks Petrov, will you please step forward?"

Katia takes a deep breath and releases my hand. Anatol tries not to grin in a manner unbecoming to a prince and fails. Sasha practically peels Feliks's fingers off her arm. She gives him a little shove, and he joins Katia beside the queen.

"For their part in my rescue, and for their service to their country, I hereby confer upon Katia Feodora and Feliks Petrov full pardons. They are now, and from this day forward, free citizens of Demidova."

At that, Katia takes in a little breath that I think might be a sob.

A great roar goes up from the crowd, and Feliks looks up at Katia with such wonder on his face that I know exactly how Sasha feels when I hear her sniffle.

The queen bids everyone to enjoy the feast, but the people are still standing and cheering as she steps down from the fountain and leads the procession back into the palace. Father is at her side, still holding Mother's hand, so Sasha and I wait for Feliks and Katia, who are the last to step down. Feliks gives a wary look at the guards who flank them as though he still can't believe they're escorting him and not arresting him. Katia's face is flushed vivid pink.

"All those Demidovans cheering for a Pyots'kan girl," she says when she reaches us.

"A brave, good Pyots'kan girl who's not afraid to do the right thing, even if it's hard," I say. Her face crumples and I hug her, then feel Sasha's arms go around me too.

When we step back into the palace, everyone chimes their glasses. I wish I had one, but then I wonder whether I might break it if I did, because I'm squeezing Feliks's and Katia's hands hard enough that it almost hurts. Sasha has hold of Feliks's other hand too, so we're linked in a line.

Queen Ana smiles. "Let us take our seats."

I walk perhaps a little faster than I should towards the food, and end up level with the queen, close enough to hear her say to Lady Olegevna, "Of course we're already doing everything in our power to find out what happened at the docks. But the good news is that, thanks to Valor Raisayevna and her friends, our power is quite considerable, and we intend to keep it that way."

I find my name card, with its elegant looping script. Sasha's name is next to mine, and my heart leaps when I see Mother's name on my other side. I look for her, but she's showing Feliks and Katia to their places at the table and seems very interested in everything Feliks has to say.

The gathered crowd raises their glasses again and waits as Sasha slips into her place. Anatol sits on his mother's right-hand side, Lady Olegevna and my father on her left. Katia and Feliks still look somewhere between shocked and delighted.

The queen seats herself, and so does my mother, who takes my hand immediately.

Sasha leans in to my side. "Valor, this is all for us—for *you*."

The guests chime on their glasses. Tureens of shining glazed vegetables fill the table between crystal goblets and plates stacked with fresh bread. Steaming dishes of herb-infused meat swimming in rich gravy are placed before us all at the same time, and the serving staff takes a step back.

"To Valor!" calls Queen Ana.

"To Valor!" echo the seated courtiers lining both sides of the great table.

Mother leans in to my other side, and both she and Sasha put their arms around me.

I raise my glass towards my friends, towards their loyalty and their bravery and their new freedom.

"To Feliks and Katia," I say.

Katia's cheeks flush, and her eyes are riveted to the table until Feliks whispers something that makes her smile.

His own grin shines bright as sunlight as he raises his glass to me. Katia lifts her eyes and looks around at all the nobles and advisers with their glasses aloft—at the queen of Demidova toasting a village girl from Pyots'k. Her gaze lands on me, and her fingers venture forward to clasp her own glass.

Anatol is the first to echo my toast, catching my eye and giving me a slow nod of thanks as the whole table repeats his words. I return the nod, and it says more than any fancy speech could say.

My heart is as full as the fountain in the square outside, and when my mother holds my hand and Sasha rests her head on my shoulder, it overflows.

ACKNOWLEDGEMENTS

As ever I am so grateful to my excellent agent, Andrea Somberg, and to my brilliant editor, Hali Baumstein, whose notes are as kind as they are insightful.

To my longtime friend and critique partner, Michelle Krys, who is always there to read and reread and who is also available for opinions on wedding attire, life-changing decisions and brands of foundation.

Thanks to the wonderful team at Bloomsbury US: Sally Morgridge, Oona Patrick, Ben Holmes, Noella James, Jeanette Levy and Donna Mark (for design but also the fantastic title!), and Lizzy Mason, Anna Bernard, Erica Barmash, Emily Ritter and Beth Eller in publicity and marketing. Thanks to Torstein Nordstrand for another stunning cover illustration.

Many thanks also to the equally lovely and supportive team at Bloomsbury UK: Vicky Leech, Zöe Griffiths, Katrina

Northern, Emily Marples and Lucy Mackay-Sim. Thanks to Laura Tolton, whose beautiful art graces the cover of the UK version of the book.

To Dave, you're the very best and I love you. And to my kids, who have my whole heart.